BOOK of legion

Dust & Flowers

ja huss

BADLANDS MC
BOOK 1

Montana Badlands.
Outlaw Bikers.
Ranch Royalty.

War is coming.
Their secret just became everyone's problem.

Book of Legion - Badlands MC #1
A Dark Outlaw Biker Serial Romance
DUST
&
flowers
New York Times Bestselling Author
JA HUSS

DUST AND FLOWERS
BOOK OF LEGION — BADLANDS MC
BOOK 1

BADLANDS

ABOUT THE BOOK

Savannah Ashby has been photographed 70,000 times —every smile, every outfit, every moment of her perfect ranch heiress life has been documented on social media by her dead mother's cameras.

Legion Kane came out of Whitefall Prison with nothin' but an expired driver's license, $27 in his wallet, and a name that means biblical demon possession.

She wears another man's three-carat diamond.

He wears a fresh MC brand burned into his chest.

This star-crossed couple have been meeting in secret at an abandoned silo since they were kids.

Now her family wants him dead, his MC wants him loyal, and the only thing that matters is what happens when she meets him at midnight, whisperin' his name like a prayer.

Montana badlands.

Outlaw bikers.

Ranch royalty.

War is coming.

DUST AND FLOWERS
Their secret just became everyone's problem.

Inside the pages you can expect:
🏍️⛓️🔥 Outlaw Biker Romance
💎🖤🔧 Rich Girl / Poor Boy
⛓️🔒🖤 Property Of
🖤🔪⚔️ Morally Gray / Anti-Hero MMC
🔥👁️⛓️ Obsessed / Possessive MMC
🚫🖤👯 Forbidden Love
👰💍🖤 Only Her
🖤⚔️🤵 Only Him
💕🏠 Childhood Sweethearts
⚔️🔪💀 Touch Her and Die
🔥🌶️😳 Primal Spice
🙊🔐🖤 Secret Relationship

Dust & Flowers

Through midnight's veil I glide
with wings of coal,
My love ignites what darkness
cannot dole.
Your descent enough to make
the angels cry.
To meet me where the damned
will go to die.

You cast aside your blush
of halo flame,
I shed my cloak of
everlasting shame.
Our union breaks the cosmic
law in two,
Makes rebels of the false
and of the true.

One word between us splits
the very sky,
They come for us but still
we strive to try.
To make a place where love
can truly grow,
To Hell with those above
and those below.

LEGION

CHAPTER 1
LEGION

Hell isn't a place you go, it's a place you carry back.

That's my poetic opinion after serving three years in prison for something I didn't do.

Willingly, I might add. Not the shit I didn't do, but the shit I went in for.

But if you want my professional opinion on hell—and at this point in my life, I feel like I'm qualified to have a professional opinion—Hell is just... well, everything around you.

This world. These people. All the rules, all the traps, the entire fuckin' game is rigged.

That's hell.

It's everywhere.

But... occasionally.

Every once in a while.

There is a day like today that makes Hell not so hot.

The gates of Whitefall Prison open in front of me. Loud, and clanging as radio chatter from the guards fills the gap between this world and that one. The June morning spreads out before me in a way I've never noticed before. Bright, hot, and… oddly, empty.

One of the guards starts yappin' at me to fucking get on with it and starts the mechanism to close the gates back up as he makes pointless, hollow threats. So when I do get on with it, I pass through just before the heavy steel gates slam closed.

It's a lot of pointless drama.

Another guard heckles me from the tower when I pause, fumbling through the yellow envelope that contains pretty much everything I own at the moment —a twenty-seven-dollar cash-out from my prison account and my driver's license, two years expired— and remove a pack of Reds.

Demon this, the hecklin' guard says. *Demon that. Demon… Demon… Demon.*

Cause that's me.

Legion Kane.

We are many.

I take out a smoke, light it up using the Bic that also did time with me, suck in my freedom, and slowly distance myself from the three years of time I did, but didn't have to.

Trying to remember to appreciate it.

Inhale. A ritual to keep me standing.

Exhale. The smoke drifts up like a prayer.

I take a few steps away from the prison, no urge to look back, and just scan the world before me as I continue smoking.

It's a whole bunch of nothin'. I'm talking big sky over vast badlands and that's about it.

But it shouldn't be this way.

This parking lot should not be empty.

But I guess it checks out, because I'm early.

One day early.

What could that possibly mean? What government facility actually makes mistakes in your favor? It doesn't happen.

There should be bikes here. All lined up.

Should be brothers with cuts, and grins, and the promise of whiskey.

Badlands owes me that much.

Where the *fuck* is everyone?

As if on cue, as if this whole fucking thing is a movie, as if I was cast in the leading role of a story no one bothered to write an ending for—the wind shifts, and suddenly, in the distance, appears a white Ford F-350. Dust blowin' up behind it, catching sunlight in ways that make it look like somethin' holy.

I squint my eyes, take a drag on the smoke, and watch as it screams into the parking lot like judgment day arriving early.

One day early.

The Ashby Ranch logo gleams on the door panel—a stylized "A" with barbed wire wrapped around it. In some places, money whispers. In Eastern Montana, money announces itself with chrome trim and custom wheels.

Cash Ashby skids the truck to a stop twenty feet away. The engine idles like it's alive. Baring its teeth, waitin' to bite. He kills it with a press of a button and the silence that follows feels deliberate, like a statement.

When the driver's door swings open, his boots hit gravel with a crunch that carries weight. And it's not just a sound—it's a fuckin' proclamation. The kind that comes with land deeds, water rights, and bank accounts that never run dry.

Cash steps out, all six-four of him the product of pure Montana breeding just like the cattle he runs. His Stetson catches the morning June sun, brim pulled low, but not so low I can't see his eyes sizing me up.

What's ol' Legion been up to, that look says. *How much has he changed. How far can I push him.*

"Well goddamn, Kane. Three years looks good on you." His mouth lifts up at one corner—that half-smile that's gotten him out of bar fights and into bedroom windows across three counties. "Prison food must be better than they say."

My face plays it cool. Not because it *can't* smile, it just kinda forgot how.

"*Caaaaaash*." I drag the word out slow, lettin' my drawl thicken. "Thought the welcoming committee would have patches, not polo shirts."

Cash leans against his truck door, crossing one ostrich-leather boot over the other. Casual as a shiv between the ribs.

"So how was it really?" he asks, like he cares. "Life inside treating Legion Kane to all the amenities?"

I give him what he wants to hear. What men like Cash always want—stories that make them feel better about never having to find out for themselves.

"Oh, you know. Won the prison talent show. Twice." I pull from the cigarette, let smoke curl between us. "Food was five-star. Especially Tuesdays. Taco Tuesday in Whitefall is something spiritual. Made friends with the warden. Good man. Collects model trains and photographs of other people's wives." I flick ash toward the ground. "Got my GED. Then a PhD in theoretical physics. Wrote my thesis on the space-time implications of watching paint dry on cinder block."

Cash's eyes narrow just enough to tell me he doesn't find me funny.

Which is fair. I'm not sure a single person on this planet finds me funny.

"So what about you, Cash?" I shift the weight of my envelope, watching his eyes track the movement. "Still breakin' hearts? Or have you fucked your way through all the local fancy bitches and moved on to the rural trash?"

"Like your—" But he doesn't finish. He catches himself in a way that doesn't quite add up.

"Like my *what*?" I ask, eyes narrowing. "Were you gonna say my *mother*?" Who died nine years back? Nah. That's not what he was gonna say.

But before I can ask questions about his remark, he tilts his chin toward the passenger side of the truck and jangles his keys between fingers weathered from reins and rope, calloused in ways money can't prevent. "Need a ride?"

The question hangs between us, simple on the surface.

But nothing's simple with an Ashby.

I take stock of my options. Released one day early. Governments fuck up plenty, but not about release days.

No club here to welcome me back with a patch I earned with my silence.

Cash shows up.

Twenty-seven dollars won't get me far and walking sixty miles back to Drybone isn't my idea of a good time.

I nod once. "Sure. Appreciate it."

No eagerness, or reluctance. Just survival math.

I slide into the passenger seat, body adjusting to the smooth, soft leather. The truck is new and isn't a work truck, per se. Not with the upgrades. It was custom. So there's a big ol' screen built into the dash. Wide, and pretty, and full fuckin' color. And on that screen is a picture of Savannah Ashby, Cash's younger sister, her long hair catching the golden hour sun like an angel.

But she's not alone.

A man stands beside her, hand resting possessively on her lower back. Tailored suit. Political smile. The kind of man who's never had dirt under his fingernails that wasn't put there deliberately for a campaign photo op.

I let my eyes linger just long enough to catalog details. The way her head tilts toward him. The diamond catching light on her left hand. The careful staging of intimacy.

The photo sits prominently displayed. Impossible to miss.

Cash says nothing.

I say nothing.

The truck roars out of the parking lot the same way it came in.

Highways in Eastern Montana stretch long and far. Empty land on both sides, nothing but fence posts marking property lines that mean everything to men like Cash and nothing to men like me.

The first twenty miles pass in silence.

Not the comfortable kind. The kind that performs itself—two men who have nothing to say pretending they're just choosing not to speak.

I watch Cash's eyes flick to the rearview. Once. Twice. Third time his jaw tightens, muscle jumping beneath tanned skin. His knuckles whiten on the steering wheel.

He's worried about something.

Badlands, probably.

They're gonna be pissed about missing my release day. Three years of keeping my mouth shut, taking the fall, earning my patch—and now the welcome wagon's a no-show because Cash Ashby pulled strings to grab me first.

Why?

It's anybody's guess.

The AC hums cold against my skin. Some sad-sack country song whispers from the speakers, turned down low enough that I only catch fragments. Something about burying love next to the hunting dogs out back.

My fingers trace the edges of the letters inked across my knuckles. M-E-R-C-Y. My baby sister. Nine years old and already carrying the weight of our family's broken promises. The one person who never stopped needing me, even when I chose not to be there.

Because that's what this prison sentence was.

A choice.

I didn't do it.

And I get it, everyone says that.

But no. I really, *really* didn't do it.

I was just the cleanest motherfucker without a previous felony record within reach. A guaranteed slap on the wrist.

Three years. I mean, I guess it's a helluva lot better than twenty, but it's still three fuckin' years.

Cash clears his throat like he's about to deliver a sermon. His finger taps the photo, just sittin' there on the screen in all its loud, static stillness. "That's Marcus," he says, eyes sliding sideways to gauge my reaction.

Here it comes. The whole reason for… whatever this is we're doin' in this truck.

"Marcus White Jr. Montana State senator's son. Georgetown Law. Worked on two presidential campaigns."

I don't give him the satisfaction of a flinch.

"He and Savannah have been together almost two years now." Cash keeps talking, voice casual like we're discussing cattle prices. "Getting engaged this weekend. Big party at the ranch. Half the state's invited."

I say nothing, but I notice what he doesn't point out —the diamond already gleaming on Savannah's finger in the photo. Engagement this weekend, but she's already wearing the ring.

The photo's staged. The moment has been manufactured.

I shouldn't be surprised. She *is* Eleanor's daughter, after all. The woman who turned life into content before anyone knew what to call it.

"Look," Cash continues, emboldened by my silence, "Savannah's moved on. She's someone else's now." His voice takes on that big-brother authority that probably works on ranch hands. "She's done with all that running around you two used to do."

I stare at the highway, counting fence posts to keep from counting the ways I could make him stop talking.

"It was never gonna work out," he says, like he's explaining gravity to a child. "You know that. Hell, she knew that. Why do you think she never visited? Never wrote?"

He keeps going, laying out the particulars of a relationship he knows nothing about. The stolen nights in the grain silo. The promises whispered against skin. The way her breath caught when I put my fingers inside her.

"Marcus is good for her. Good for the family. Good for the ranch." Cash's sermon picks up steam. "He's the kind of man who builds legacies, not the kind who burns them down."

I keep my face blank. Prison teaches you that—how to wear nothing when you feel everything.

"Don't make this harder than it needs to be," Cash says finally, like he's offering wisdom instead of a threat.

And then he yanks the steering wheel hard to the right, pulling his pristine Ford F-350 onto the gravel shoulder with a spray of dust and small stones that ping against the undercarriage. The truck rocks to a stop, suspension groaning in protest, as if even the vehicle itself knows we're about to cross a line that can't be uncrossed. The engine idles with a low, threatening rumble that matches the tension thickening the air between us.

Cash shifts in his seat, adjusts his grip on the wheel.

The anger that tightened his jaw a minute ago dissolves into something worse—pity. His mouth stretches into what he probably thinks is a friendly smile. Just two men having a roadside chat.

"Let's part as friends," he says, nodding toward the dusty shoulder we're parked on. "Been a long time coming, this conversation."

Again, I stay quiet. The silence burns between us.

He takes my stillness as an invitation. "You know, I've been thinking about where things went wrong with you. Why you never really learned your place." He taps his fingers against the wheel, thoughtful, like he's solving a puzzle. "I blame myself, really. Should've set you straight about my baby sister when it first got out of hand."

My jaw locks tight enough to crack teeth. The rage comes fast—a familiar burn that starts in my gut and climbs my spine.

"I found some pictures," he says.

Well, fuck.

"Yeah," Cash says. Gauging my reaction. "And do you know what those pictures were of?"

Well, of course, I do. Because I was there. But I don't say that because… well, some things are just better left unsaid. Also, I've got no idea which pictures he's specifically talking about.

Eleanor Ashby, Cash and Savannah's mother—probably the most famous photographer on the fuckin' planet at one point—literally took hundreds, hell, maybe even thousands, of pictures of me.

"Well, I'll tell you then, just in case you think I'm bluffing. Those pics were of you and Savannah."

"Ohhh… kaaaay."

"OK?" Cash is pissed now. "She was fourteen fucking years old."

Ah. There's the clue I needed. "What were we doin' in those pics, Cash?" I only ask because I know. When Savannah was fourteen, I was sixteen. And we'd only been hanging out two years at that point.

That's how long it took me to kiss her.

Two years.

"You were kissing her," he says. But it comes out almost a whisper. Like he's saying something dirty.

"Kissin' her. That's what you're pissed about? Because we kissed when we were kids?"

"I wanted to kill you," Cash sneers. Malice now. He can't control it anymore. "But Eleanor wouldn't let me handle it."

Of course, she wouldn't. His mother loved me far more than she ever loved him.

She never told him that—I'm sure of it. Hell, she never told me either.

But you *know*. You *know* when someone loves you just like you know when they don't.

"She said it was just a phase," Cash says. "Said Savannah needed to learn some lessons the hard way."

This is interesting and actually explains quite a lot about why Cash Ashby has always hated me, even though our paths never connected in any meaningful way. We didn't go to school together, we didn't hang out together, we didn't do shit together.

The only thing we had in common was Savannah. And what Savannah and I had was a secret.

Well, not so secret, I guess. I knew Eleanor was

taking pictures of us. She told me. Well, showed me, actually.

But I had no idea that Cash knew.

Savannah certainly didn't. Not about these pictures Cash is referring to now, or any of the others Eleanor kept locked away.

"I mean, what did you think was gonna happen?" Cash continues, warming to the subject now. "That you'd ride up on that piece-of-shit motorcycle, and she'd throw everything away? The ranch? The family name? The inheritance? For what—some trailer trash with a GED and a criminal record?"

Outside the window, the land stretches empty in all directions. No cars. No houses. Just dust, and distance, and the fading line of asphalt cutting through it all.

"You were a distraction," Cash says, voice lower now. "A little rebellion she needed to get out of her system. But she's done with that now. Done with you."

I open the door without a word, swing my legs out. The heat hits me like a wall—dry, punishing Montana summer. Dust kicks up around my boots as they hit the gravel.

Cash leans across the seat, still smiling that empty smile. "Forty miles to Drybone. I'd start walking if I were you."

I shut the door with just enough force to be heard, not enough to give him the satisfaction of my anger. The window rolls down, and Cash's face appears in the opening, smug and certain.

"Oh, and Legion? Don't bother showing up at the engagement party. Security has your picture."

I stand still as the truck pulls away, tires spitting

gravel that stings against my legs. The red taillights shrink to pinpricks, then vanish around a bend. The silence that follows feels like a held breath—the whole world on pause. Waiting.

No cars in either direction.

Just highway and heat waves shimmering off asphalt.

Expired driver's license.

Twenty-seven dollars.

Half a pack of cigarettes.

A Bic.

No phone.

No water.

Forty miles to Drybone.

I start walking.

CHAPTER 2
LEGION

Forty miles might as well be four hundred as the Montana summer sun beats down, hot and merciless. It doesn't care who you are or what you've done—it burns everyone the same.

My jeans hang loose after three years of prison food and too much time to work out, but the white t-shirt sticks to my back, filled out with muscles I never even knew existed before pull-ups became a ritual. My brown biker boots still fit and feel like home, but not meant for walking.

So this walk gets old fast.

The first mile passes in a blur of numb thoughts and burning skin.

By mile three, my throat feels like I swallowed sandpaper.

By mile five, I've gone through two cigarettes, saving the rest. Not much else to ration.

By mile seven, I'm thinking about all the ways to kill a man with a Stetson hat.

The sun climbs higher, past merciful and into cruel. I pull my shirt off, using it to wipe sweat from my face before tucking it into my back pocket. The ink across my chest and arms drinks in the heat—the archangel over my heart, the bone court on my left pectoral, the scorch line climbing my ribs. Prison art layered over older work, a history of bad decisions written in permanent ink.

Three hours in, I figure I've done about ten miles. Only thirty more to go.

I almost laugh at that. *Almost.*

A distant rumble builds behind me—the first vehicle I've heard since Cash's truck disappeared. I don't bother turning or sticking out my thumb. No one stops for men who look like me.

But the semi slows anyway, air brakes hissing, wheels kicking up dust as the truck slows down next to me, coming to a stop. The passenger window slides down. I have to take several steps back to see the man inside. "Where you headed?" he calls out. Older guy, maybe sixty, with a beard gone mostly gray and eyes that have seen enough highway to circle the earth.

"Drybone."

He nods once. "Hop in."

I hesitate, just for a second. In prison, nothing comes free.

"Ain't got all day," he says, not unkindly.

But even if this old man was a serial killer, I'd still accept the ride. Be stupid not to. So I haul myself up and the AC hits me like salvation, cold enough to raise goosebumps on my sun-baked skin.

"Name's Earl," he says, putting the rig in gear.

"Legion."

He gives me a look. "That what your mama called you?"

"That's what everyone calls me."

Earl nods like that answers more than his question. "Only thing out this way is Whitefall," he says, eyes back on the road. "How many years did ya do?"

"Three."

"Could've been worse, then."

Yup. That's my philosophy too. It can always get worse.

I turn toward the window, watchin' the land roll by at sixty-five instead of three miles an hour. Earl doesn't push for conversation, just reaches into a cooler between the seats and hands me a bottle of water without comment.

The cold plastic feels unreal in my hand. I drink half in one go, forcing myself to cap it before I make myself sick.

Then… well, now that I'm not fixated on dyin' of heatstroke on a barren highway, my mind drifts to Savannah.

Always Savannah.

It's always been Savannah.

The angel to my demon.

I was fourteen the first time I ever got her all to myself. She was twelve. She found the old grain silo on her pony, I was on my bike. It was a regular place for me. Situated somewhere right along the boundary of ours and theirs.

Which makes us sound like neighbors, and technically, I guess we were. But there were twenty acres of Kane land and about three hundred of Ashby land between the two parcels. Let's just say, our mailboxes didn't stand side-by-side on the road.

So I'd found that old silo years before she ever had the pony, or permission, to get herself out exploring that far from home. It was late summer, the time of year when the heat hangs so thick you can taste it. My BMX had a rusted frame and brakes that only worked when they felt like it. The chain slipped if you pedaled too hard, so I learned to ride gentle even when I wanted to tear through the world.

I wasn't looking for anything that day. Just moving along. Getting away from the trailer because my teenage life was a fuckin' mess. Step-dad, Deacon, was working double shifts and my mama was home, pregnant with my middle sister, Destiny.

The idea of my baby sister, Mercy, wouldn't appear for nine more years.

It was a weird time. Still an only child, but not really. Deacon didn't take much notice of me. I'm not sure why. Maybe I'm just uninterestin'. Maybe I was just never worth his time. Whatever it was, he left me alone.

Not my mama, though. He bullied her pretty good and by the time she was pregnant and I was fourteen, I'd had enough. Started mouthin' back. I wasn't big, not yet. But Deacon could see the writing on that wall. I *would* be big. And he didn't want any part of that.

It wasn't that I didn't care about the way he treated my mama, it was just a consequence of her own choices. She was a grown woman, for fuck's sake. I was a child.

She knew better than anyone that Deacon was an asshole.

But sometimes, when life is cruel, ya just hold your nose and make due. The cold, hard fact is that she needed his money. Asshole, yes. Deadbeat… I mean, I hate to say it. I'm not a Deacon supporter, but the man always kept a job. And nah, he didn't make good money. But at least he paid the bills.

Anyway. On that day, the day I first had Savannah Ashby's full attention, I went out to the old silo because there was a creek there that actually ran—trickle of a thing as it was.

There was a pony tied to the fence post when I got there. Buckskin, with a saddle that look both old and expensive at the same time. I don't claim to be a horse expert, but it's pretty easy to identify the ones that worked hard and slept under the stars and the ones that didn't. Lots of kids out here had horses and ponies. Most of them caked in dirt, even when well cared for.

This little buckskin was shiny and clean.

I don't remember its name. Savannah had lots of ponies and horses over the years. They came and went, most of them.

But this was the first of them for me. It was just standin' there, right outside the cutaway door in the old metal silo, grazing on scrub.

Inside the silo, Savannah was singing.

That's how it all started.

Me and my BMX, her and her pony.

And that voice. Like an angel.

She didn't hear me, or if she did, it wasn't enough to make her stop singing. When I stepped inside the silo the sunlight was streaming through the cracks cuttin' the dust into thin gold blades and Savannah

Ashby was sitting on the upper platform, legs dangling off, her dress ruffles fluttering as she swung her feet. She was even wearing white. Dress, cowboy boots, and the cowboy hat on her head were all soaking up the dusty sunlight like she was the definition of a good girl.

The song was Ave Maria. I'd heard it before, but never like this. I almost backed out of the silo without sayin' nothin' because kids like me didn't breathe the same air as kids like her.

But she'd already seen me. She stopped singing and said, "Ain't it loud in here with nothin' in it?"

Her voice was all Ashby polish wrapped around long vowels. And these sounds hung in the air—or, at the very least, in my mind—like church bells that vibrate long after they've been rung.

"Yeah," I told her back, because I couldn't think of anything smarter to say.

We already knew each other, sorta. Same town. Same church, sometimes. But she went to private school a few towns over, only home on weekends. There wasn't a moment in my life when Savannah Ashby wasn't in it.

But it was in a distant way.

Nothing somethin' this up close and personal. That meetin' right there was the first time we were ever *alone* together. The first time we ever talked.

She sang a little more. All church songs. All songs I knew, if only by osmosis.

And I sat on the lower rungs of the ladder, elbows on my knees, sweaty from my ride explorin'. She stayed on the edge of the platform, swinging her feet and twirling a piece of hay between her fingers like it held answers.

We talked about siblings. My new one upcomin' and her older brothers. She had three—of course, I knew this. Everyone knows the Ashby brothers. Cash, Wyatt, and Colt in descending order.

We talked about her being watched by her mother's camera lens. I understood—fuckin Eleanor watched me too. But I didn't say nothin' about that to Savannah. I could relate though, that was the important part.

We talked about growin' up in a town where everyone knew your name.

Hers, and how she would elevate it.

Mine, and how I was gonna ruin it.

I knew Eleanor much better than I knew Savannah back then. Eleanor Ashby was a very famous photographer and the Little Ashby Princess was the subject of every single published photo.

Every single bit of Savannah's life was online. I didn't look at it back then. I didn't have a phone to check socials. Didn't want a phone to check socials. Still don't have any fuckin' socials.

But other kids did. So I'd seen my share of those photos.

Eleanor didn't put me online. She said I was somethin' else. Photogenic. The most beautiful child she'd ever seen, is what she really told me—*hundreds* of times.

But Legion Kane was a story nobody really wanted to hear about.

I was too poor to put on a magazine cover.

It was never my face online—just Savannah's.

Every day, three, four, five, six times a day Eleanor posted a picture or two of her perfect little princess.

She took pictures of me everywhere as well. Riding my bike, running around the county fair, coming out of school. There isn't a place within fifty miles of Drybone, Montana that Eleanor Ashby didn't find me and take a fuckin' picture.

Even came to the trailer once. On a pretense, of course. My mama never knew about the photos. Deacon wasn't my daddy, so whether he knew or not, no one cared.

So I knew the Ashbys the way other folks around here know them—from afar.

But also, from the other end of Eleanor's camera lens.

And I knew Savannah in that first way as well.

But on this day, I knew her in a different way.

I had her all to myself that day.

And that's where it all started.

Innocently, of course. It would be a year before we held hands. Two before I kissed her. And three years, almost to the day, before we made it all official by losing our virginity together. I was seventeen, she was fifteen, and it was perfect.

We never dated.

Nah. Just hookups.

That's all I was to them—the Ashbys. Something to be seen through a lens. Something to be held at a distance.

. . .

The truck hits a pothole, jolting me back to the here and now. The memory fades, but the ache doesn't.

I stare out the window, watching Montana blur past. I was a different person back then. We both were. Before the ink on my skin, before the blood on my hands, before prison walls and engagement rings.

But the relationship stuck, that's for sure.

The next week after that first meetin', I gave Savannah a pocketknife with my initials scratched off. She let me brush her pony. We didn't tell anyone. We didn't have to.

We just kept meeting—no lies, no pressure. No one taking pictures.

Just two kids sitting in a silo where the silence wasn't empty, it was safe.

Now, nothing's safe.

Not the memories or my future.

Earl drops me at the crossroads with a friendly honk, dust billowing behind his eighteen wheels as he pulls away. I tip an imaginary hat at his taillights and continue my walk.

The sun's still high enough to burn, but I can see the shade of the cottonwoods ahead where the old riverbed cuts between Kane scrub and Ashby wealth. I turn toward it like a man following his religion.

Two miles to my trailer. Two miles of memory and dust.

The dry riverbed is a wound in the earth that only bleeds water three months a year. Spring makes it something else entirely—rushing snowmelt carving through soft banks, wildflowers nodding heavy on the edges. Water so cold it burns your feet when you wade in. Used to dare Destiny to cross it during the flood season, watching her balance on slippery rocks while I pretended not to be ready to dive in after her.

I step down the crumbling bank, boots sliding in loose dirt. The cottonwoods stand like sentinels on both sides, their leaves whispering secrets above me. They've been here longer than any Ashby, longer than any Kane. Their roots drink deep from water that's still there, hidden under the baked clay and stones.

This place was everything once. Territory line. Playground. Baptism pool—figuratively, of course.

I kick at a smooth river stone, watch it skitter across the cracked earth. Used to skip these across rushing water, teaching Mercy how to count the bounces. Five was our record. Five perfect skips before the current took it.

Cash's words crawl through my head like wasps looking for somewhere soft to sting. *She's changed. You're just a phase she outgrew.*" His face when he said it —half-smirk, half-warning. Like he was doin' me a favor by cutting me loose before I embarrassed myself.

The staged photograph burns behind my eyes. Savannah with her perfect smile, leaning into that man with his politician's jawline and manicured hands.

I wonder if he knows how she tastes after swimming in this riverbed. If he's ever seen her with mud up to her knees and her hair wild in the wind. If he knows she can sing "Ave Maria" so sweet it makes your chest ache.

I doubt it. Men like him don't love women—they acquire them.

The engagement party is nothing but a moment to be curated.

But I get it. When Eleanor died, she left everything to Savannah. Out of guilt, maybe. For takin' all those pictures and erasing any hope of Savannah ever having a private life. But it came with conditions.

"It says I have to marry respectable."

"What the hell does that mean?" I understood what it meant, I just wanted to hear her say it.

"It means I can't marry you, Legion. Not if I want the Estate to exist."

I can't marry you, Legion.

As if this was something we had discussed.

It wasn't. We never dated. We fucked. A lot, some years. A lot less, some others.

Never, not for a single fuckin' second, did I ever think I would *marry* Savannah Ashby.

So… I guess that's where Marcus Jr whatever comes in.

Respectable.

Engagement party.

Everyone in Drybone will be there, dressed in their Sunday best, drinking champagne they can't afford, watching the Ashby princess fulfill the requirements in Eleanor's will. Marry rich. Marry respectable. Marry anyone but the trash from across the dry riverbed.

Savannah Ashby's life has been choreographed from start to finish, courtesy of Eleanor. And Eleanor *knew* what I meant to Savannah. How much Savannah meant to *me.*

And still, she spelled it out.

She *spelled it out.*

What the actual fuck.

I'm not even sure I can explain what it feels like when a woman you kinda, sorta, liked and trusted, threatens her daughter with generational poverty if she so much as thinks about marrying my biker ass.

Engagement party.

What a fuckin' joke.

I reach the middle of the riverbed and stop, looking up at the blue slice of sky between cottonwood branches. On my right, twenty acres of Kane scrubland with a rusted trailer sinking into dust. On my left, the endless green pastures of the Ashby Ranch, where sprinklers run even in drought years, courtesy of artesian wells.

Water rights are like magic around here.

So. I guess Savannah made her choice. Got the ring to prove it.

Never mind that I know her better than I know the ink on my skin. That I've tasted the salt on her cheeks when she cries. That I've heard confessions she'd never tell a priest. That I've held her while she shook with rage at her mother's cameras, and fucked her softly under the starlight.

Never mind all that, Legion.

She's moved on…

Cash can warn me all he wants. That Marcus guy can buy her diamonds big as her knuckles.

But I'm willing to bet my last twenty-seven dollars that if I show up at that engagement party, Savannah won't turn me away. The girl who met me in an abandoned grain silo for six years is still in there somewhere, behind the perfect smile and designer dress.

And I'm not quite ready to give her up.

Because if there's one thing I've learned while inside, it's this: You get one shot in this life.

And that one shot translates to one precious, fleeting fucking moment when everything hangs in the balance —when the scales could tip either way and your whole future stretches out before you like a highway with two very different destinations.

One shot.

Don't miss.

Because if you miss it, if you hesitate for even a heartbeat too long, that road disappears forever, leaving nothing but dust and regret where the possibility once lived.

One shot.

I don't miss.

CHAPTER 3
LEGION

The Kane Family Legacy is twenty acres of shitty scrubland and a trailer that's more rust than metal.

Home sweet fucking home.

And when I crest the hill and it comes in to view, it doesn't welcome me back, just reminds me of why I left. The aluminum siding's peelin' off in strips, like it's a snake instead of a trailer. Shedding its own skin. The front steps sag worse than before, wooden boards warped from decades of weather. Weeds as tall as my knees crowd the walkway, and a tumbleweed has wedged itself between the propane tank and what's left of the skirting. The mailbox tilts sideways, mouth hanging open like it gave up years ago. Nothing but spiders living there now.

Three years, and it's aged twenty.

Proof that time doesn't heal all wounds.

Sometimes it just makes them uglier.

I stop ten feet from the steps, listening as the wind

pushes through the tall grass. Metal creaks somewhere —roof or siding, hard to tell.

No human sounds.

"Mercy?"

Nothing. And in a place like this, silence is its own kind of scream.

The windows are intact, which surprises me. Expected them to be broken, or at least cracked. Destiny must have kept things together for longer than I thought.

I take a step toward the porch, and that's when I hear it—the soft metallic click of a BB gun being cocked.

I freeze. Not because I'm afraid of getting shot by a BB. But because I know exactly who's holding it.

"That you, Mercy?" I keep my voice easy, hands visible at my sides.

There's a rustle from the overgrown juniper bush to my left and then, she emerges like some wild thing with tangled hair and a dirty face with eyes that burn with something between fury and fear.

My baby sister. Nine years old and pointing a Red Ryder at my chest like she means business.

Children shouldn't have to be their own army, but where we come from, we don't get a choice.

She's thinner than she should be. Jeans torn at both knees, t-shirt faded to nothing. Her dark hair's a rat's nest, hanging past her shoulders. No one's been brushing it. No one's been taking care of anything.

But it's her blue, feral eyes that gut me. They are old, and watchful, and don't belong on a nine-year-old. Some kids lose their childhood. Others have it stolen. Mercy had hers murdered.

"You plannin' on shootin' me, or you just sayin' hello?"

She doesn't answer. Doesn't lower the gun either. Just stares at me with those eyes that mirror mine—Kane eyes, our mother called them. Too sharp for their own good.

"Where's Destiny?" I ask.

Nothing. Not even a blink. Which is fair, I guess. Trust isn't given freely when survival depends on keeping strangers at gunpoint.

"You been here alone?"

The BB gun wavers slightly. Her knuckles are white around the grip. I crouch down slow, getting to her eye level without coming closer. "I'm back now, Mercy. For good. You can put down the gun."

She shifts her weight, bare feet in the dirt. She thinks I'm a liar and there's not much I can do about that thirty seconds in.

So I tell her, "You don't have to talk. But I'm stayin'."

The gun lowers an inch. Her expression gives nothin' away. A perfect poker face.

It's clear now, what three years inside cost. Not just me. Her. The price she paid for my loyalty to Badlands. That's life, though. One way or the other, every choice we make writes itself on someone else's skin.

Mercy takes a step back toward the trailer, gun still raised. Testing if I'll follow. Testing if I'm real, maybe. I don't move. Let her set the pace. Let her decide if I'm worth trusting again.

"I'm stayin'," I say again. "Ya can't get rid of me that easy."

Her eyes never leave mine. No words. No welcome.

Just a child who's forgotten how to be a child, standing guard over a kingdom of dust and broken promises.

I head towards the steps, feelin' the need to get this shit over with. To see what I'm comin' back to. To see what's left of this piece-of-shit broken place.

Inside, the trailer smells like... something I can't place at first. Not rot or mold. Not exactly clean either. Just... lived in.

Different than I remember.

Mercy comes in behind me, edging past the kitchen counter, keeping her back to the wall, eyes never leaving mine. Smart girl. Never turn your back on what you don't trust.

I glance around, cataloging what's changed and what hasn't. The couch still sags in the middle, threadbare arms worn to the foam. Coffee table's got new scratches. Kitchen sink has dishes in it—not many, but enough to show someone's been eating here.

But there are fresh groceries on the counter. Not much. A loaf of bread that isn't moldy, milk that's still cold, peanut butter, and some apples.

I look over at the corner that acts like a dining room and spot some clean clothes. Folded neatly in stacks of t-shirts and pants. Mercy-sized. Too neat for this nine-year-old to have done herself.

"Where's Destiny?" I ask, turning back to Mercy.

Mercy shakes her head once, quick and definite.

"She here?" I press.

Mercy just stares, her face a blank wall.

I move past her toward the hallway. "I'm gonna check the rooms."

Every door you open in your childhood home

shows you who you used to be, and these doors are no different.

The trailer has three bedrooms—if you can call them that. More like closets with doors. I check Destiny's room first. Door's unlocked. I push it open to find... nothing much. Bed's still there, dresser too. But the walls are bare. No clothes in the closet. No sign anyone's slept here in months.

"When did she leave?" I ask over my shoulder.

No answer from Mercy, who's hovering in the hallway, watching me.

I push open the door to my room. It's exactly as I left it three years ago—bed still made with military corners, empty walls, nothing personal here. Not one damn thing because this old trailer was never 'home'.

And in the center of the linoleum floor, a dead mouse, dried to leather.

It stares back at me, those blank, black, beady eyes, as if to say, welcome home, Legion.

Some homecomings are celebrations.

Others are funerals for the life you thought you'd return to.

I back out of my room, leaving the dead mouse as a memorial to what happens when you disappear for three years. Some things just shrivel up and die when you're not there to keep them breathing.

Not that I had any responsibility to the local rodents, but an omen is an omen.

Back out in the hallway the walls press in and the whole place just feels small and completely insignificant. Mercy trails behind me, her bare feet silent on the linoleum. That BB gun's still in her hands, but pointed down now.

Progress, I guess.

"Who's been feeding you?" I ask.

Mercy just stares at me.

"Who brought the groceries, Mercy?"

She's not gonna answer.

She doesn't need to answer. I already know who it was.

"I need some air," I mutter, and go back outside where the afternoon sun beats down like judgment. I cross the yard to the old oak tree that holds the remnants of a tire swing, then run my fingers over the bark, finding what I'm looking for about chest height. The carving I made when I was fifteen.

S + L

Only it no longer says that. Cause it's been crossed out with deep gashes. Not weathered cuts, either. Recent ones.

"She was mad at you."

Mercy's voice startles me. She's standing a few feet away, BB gun held loose at her side.

I turn to face her. "Savannah did this?"

Mercy nods, then looks away. "You make her sad."

I made Savannah promise not to write me because it was over. Like, moved-on kind of over.

She moved, I moved on.

Except, we got this love that doesn't quite know how to move on.

So fine. She was mad. I make her sad.

Now she's engaged. Or will be as soon as that party happens. So… yeah.

Over.

"How often does she come?" I ask, keeping my voice neutral.

Mercy shifts her weight, looking less feral now that she's talking. "Twice a month, mostly." She picks at a scab on her elbow. "More after Destiny left."

"When did Destiny leave?"

"Two months ago." Mercy looks up at me, her eyes suddenly older than nine. "She's pregnant."

"Uh huh." The Kane family curse: we break everything we touch, including ourselves.

I scrub a hand over my face, feeling three days of stubble and a lifetime of failure. I'm supposed to be the one who protects them. Some fucking job I've done.

I go back inside, head straight for the landline mounted on the kitchen wall, and punch in the number I've had memorized since I was eighteen.

It rings twice before a gruff voice answers. "Yeah?"

"It's Legion."

A pause, then: "Holy shit! Kane! Where the fuck are you, brother?"

Brotherhood. It's the family you choose when blood fails you. And this man right here—Diesel, he's never failed me. All of a sudden, clarity hits and it comes in the form of background noise. Pool balls clacking, men laughing, music playing.

"I'm at home," I say. For the first time today, I feel something like relief. "Got out a day early."

I feel somethin' like… *belonging*. These men—whatever else they are—they're my brothers. They'd kill for me. Die for me.

"Bring me my bike," I tell Diesel. And now, it's time

to feel the freedom. To really feel what it means to walk out of that cage I put myself in. "And hey," I add, before Diesel ends the call. "Bring an extra helmet for my sister."

I hang up and turn to find Mercy watching me, something like hope in her eyes. Which is a really dangerous emotion because it makes you believe in second chances.

"Pack a bag. We're not staying here tonight."

Her eyes widen. "Where are we going?"

"Somewhere safe."

Mercy disappears down the hall as I step outside and light a smoke.

I breathe in failure. Breathe out reality.

Because fuck this place.

And fuck Savannah too.

Maybe she did come here. Maybe she did take care of Mercy.

But she's wearing another man's ring and I'm not fourteen anymore.

I deserve better. Love doesn't wait. Never waits. But I think I deserve more than some jacked-up posturing from Cash as her only goodbye.

Some chapters end with periods.

Others end with matches.

And I have a very strong urge to light this love up and watch it burn.

CHAPTER 4
SAVANNAH

The sun hangs low against the backdrop of the barn, the golden hour at hand. I stand at my bedroom window, bathing in the dying light.

This bedroom has been mine since the day I was born. Second floor, east wing. From my vantage point, the Ashby mansion looms over our expansive property. Three stories of reclaimed wood and glass, every beam hand-selected by my great-grandfather, every window positioned to frame the mountains like they belong to us.

Which they kinda do. Everything here belongs to us.

Forty-seven thousand acres of Montana that answers only to my last name.

The pastures stretch toward the horizon, dotted with Black Angus cattle that have better nutrition than ninety-nine percent of the humans on this planet.

The dark brown fences cut shadows through green fields and the barn stands in a magnificent contrast of red paint weathered to rusty-rose. The doors alone tell a story. Tall and wide, with more windows than most homes, you can drive a wagon right in to the fifteen thousand square feet our horses call home.

My first pony lived in the third stall. A dappled gray named Moonstone. My cart with the yellow wheels is still hanging from the rafters.

The whole fuckin' place feels like a museum with me, and my life, as the centerpiece. Choreographed moments, carefully curated for public display.

There are twenty-seven cameras in the barn. *Every* moment.

Even to this day, the cameras still function, though Mama has been gone seven years already.

I've been photographed in this barn close to seventy-thousand times.

Even so, the barn was the beginning of my freedom. The moment I was allowed to ride Moonstone alone, I left the Ashby mansion. The backs of my ponies and horses through the years were just as public as any playhouse or stall—but ya see, to a child on a ranch, having a pony is much like having a car.

You can go anywhere.

All by yourself.

And I did.

Running away into the hills was the only way I got through my childhood under the lens of notoriety. Precious hours spent being myself. No perfect smiles. Just dirt under my nails and hay in my hair.

It was the only way I survived.

So I love the barn. But that's not what I'm lookin' at

right now. It's the white tent just to the right of the barn that has captured my attention. This tent swallows up everything else. Not really the size of it—though there are three hundred chairs perfectly positioned around tables draped in linen. It's the… gravitas of the whole thing. There are crystal chandeliers hanging from canvas peaks and the dozens of waitstaff move like ants between the kitchen and the lawn in their black and white uniforms.

My engagement party.

A real Ashby production sponsored by "Marry Respectable".

The kind of event that gets a twelve-page spread in Vogue.

The kind of party where people fly in on private jets just to say they were there.

In the glass, I check my outfit. Smoothing my hands down my cream pencil skirt as the fluttery blouse with its tangerine floral pattern catches the last light. Lucchese boots—off-white with hand-stitched detail—peek out beneath the hem of my skirt. I'm not sure everyone would agree that cowboy boots and pencil skirts go together, but these boots were made to last, unlike most things in my life.

Turning from the window, I face the wall of photographs. My whole life, documented frame by frame. Baby Savannah in a sunbeam. Toddler Savannah with cake-smeared cheeks. Teenage Savannah on horseback, long blonde hair streaming out behind her like a banner.

All of them perfect.

None of them real.

Mama's work. Eleanor Ashby's greatest creation.

Me.

It's funny, because I miss her with an ache that feels like hunger, but I hate her with a clarity that rings like crystal. In the same moment, I miss her again because grief isn't linear and neither is love.

"There you are." Colt leans in the doorway, dressed in a tailored suit that makes his shoulders look broad and strong. My brother. Only a year older. The only one who knows what it was like to grow up as Eleanor's second-favorite project.

"You look beautiful," he says, stepping into the room. His eyes—a dark and deep Ashby blue, just like mine, sweep over me with approval. "But people are starting to ask questions, Savannah. Marcus is looking for you."

Of course he is. Marcus is always lookin' for me when I'm not where he expects me to be.

"I know Legion is out," I say, instead of answering. The words taste dangerous on my tongue. Like saying his name might summon him. If only. "I went by the trailer. It's empty."

Even Mercy is gone. That skinny little ghost of a girl with her too-old eyes and her too-young face. Gone with her brother, I suppose.

"So he came back and got her," Colt says, not asking. "Took her where?"

That's what I wanna know. Where did he go? Did he leave Drybone? Did he find someone while he was inside? Some woman who writes letters and waits for men who've done terrible things?

Maybe.

It costs me a lot to admit that.

A piece of my heart actually cracks open.

But it's just to prepare myself for my inevitable future and has little to do with Legion ever actually… replacing me.

We're… kind of a thing.

"The clubhouse," I say, certain as sunrise. "He's at the clubhouse and he took Mercy with him."

Which is no place for a nine-year-old girl. But then, neither was that falling-down trailer with its empty cupboards and broken locks. Neither was being left alone while everyone who should have protected her, disappeared one by one.

I sigh, my shoulders dropping an inch. "I'm coming."

Colt, the only Ashby brother who always takes my side, nods and steps away to let me pass.

He never judges, though he probably should.

He never lectures, though I could probably use one now and then.

He only sees and hears me. The real me. The sad me.

My heels click against the hardwood as I walk toward the stairs. Each step takes me closer to the future I'm supposed to want.

Colt doesn't follow. Will probably show up later, but he hates the jail cell this mansion has become just as much as I do.

That's why I can talk about Legion with him.

He gets me in a way that neither Wyatt nor Cash ever will.

Outside, the night air wraps around me like silk. Warm enough for bare shoulders, cool enough that goosebumps rise on my skin. The fairy lights strung between trees cast everything in gold. The white tent glows from within, making shadows dance across the outside.

Three hundred people waiting to celebrate the union of two families.

Two fortunes.

Two futures.

And there he is—Marcus White Jr., golden boy of Montana politics. Georgetown Law. Son of Montana State Senator White. Future congressman, if his father has anything to say about it.

He sees me and smiles that campaign-poster smile. Perfect teeth. Perfect hair. Perfect life waiting to fold me into it.

His lips find my neck as I reach him. Warm and soft and nothing like I want.

I close my eyes and see ink instead of skin. Black lines etched across muscle. Angels and demons locked in eternal battle. A map of scars and stories I used to trace with my fingertips in the dark.

Legion's tattoos.

Legion's body.

Legion's ghost, haunting me even here, even now, with another man's ring on my finger and the only future I ever wanted quickly slippin' away like the inheritance money the Estate will never get if I don't 'marry proper'.

Inside the massive party tent on the Ashby Ranch lawn, I hold a flute of champagne that I haven't sipped.

Marcus introduces me to another circle of nodding faces —his father's business associates, a state judge, his wife, and two lawyers whose names I hear, but don't remember.

They all wear the same expression: calculation wrapped in politeness.

"My future wife," Marcus says, his hand possessive at my waist. "Savannah Ashby."

I smile the smile Mama taught me. Lips curved just enough, teeth barely showing. The smile that says I'm listening when I'm not.

These people don't see me. They see followers. Engagement metrics. The Ashby water rights. The land that stretches farther than their imported cars can drive in a day.

"Savannah's platform reaches over four million people," Marcus explains, like I'm a television network instead of a person. "Her influence in the rural demographic is unparalleled."

The judge's wife nods, her diamond earrings catching the light. "Such a blessing for your campaign."

My gaze drifts past them to the long gravel driveway curving between the cottonwoods. I imagine headlights cutting through darkness. Not the soft purr of German engineering, but the growl of a motorcycle engine that sounds like a threat.

I imagine Legion walking across the perfect lawn toward this perfect tent. Leather-clad and dangerous. Knuckles still bruised from prison yard fights. Tattoos climbing up his throat like prayers that got twisted into curses.

These polished people would scatter like frightened birds. Their champagne flutes abandoned. Their fake smiles frozen.

"Savannah?"

Marcus's voice pulls me back. His eyes narrow slightly. He's noticed my attention wandering.

"Would you excuse me?" I say, placing my untouched champagne on a passing waiter's tray. "Just need to freshen up."

I feel Marcus watching as I walk away. He always watches. Tracks my movements like I'm an investment that might depreciate if left unattended.

Inside the carriage house, the powder room is a sanctuary of cream marble and subtle lighting. I lock the door behind me and lean against it, eyes closed, letting the quiet wrap around me.

And then I'm not here anymore.

I'm fifteen again, climbing the rusted ladder inside the abandoned grain silo. The metal cold against my palms. My heart hammering with anticipation, not dread.

Legion waiting at the top, a shadow against shadows until I got close enough to see his eyes. It was a hot summer night, but it was dark like winter. He reached for my hand, pulled me onto the platform where we'd been meeting for three years.

But that night was different.

That night, he spread his leather jacket on the wooden planks. That night, his hands shook when they touched my face.

"You sure?" he asked, his voice rough at the edges.

I answered by taking his hand and placing it over my heart. Over the lace of my bra. My skin burning everywhere he touched.

He eased me down on his jacket, the leather still warm from his body. His calloused hands moved over me like I was something sacred. Something he'd been starving for.

His lips traced a path from my throat to my breasts until I couldn't breathe right.

Couldn't think right.

Could only *feel right*.

"I've been dyin' for you," he whispered against my inner thigh, his breath hot and desperate. Then his mouth claimed me, tasting places no one had ever touched, and I practically sobbed his name into the darkness as I begged him to never stop.

When he finally pushed inside me, he went slow and careful despite the trembling in his arms. His eyes never left mine as he angled deeper, filling an emptiness I'd never acknowledged until that moment.

He moved inside me like a man both worshipping and drowning. Like he'd found religion in the arch of my back. Like salvation lived in the space between my legs.

I lean forward, gripping the marble countertop, my engagement ring catching the light as I try to steady my breathing. The memory is too vivid. Too close. I can almost feel the splinters from the wooden platform digging into my shoulders, the weight of him pressing me down, the way my body stretched to accommodate him.

The knock on the door startles me back to the present.

"Savannah? Are you all right in there?" Senator White's voice, my future father-in-law, concerned but practiced. The kind of concern that's performative, meant to be overheard and noted.

"Just a minute," I call back, running cold water over my wrists.

I check my reflection. Flushed cheeks. Bright eyes. A woman remembering things she shouldn't.

I open the door to find Marcus's father waiting, his political smile firmly in place. "The Daleworths were asking after you. They're considering a substantial donation to Marcus's exploratory committee."

Of course they are. That's what this party is really about. Not my engagement. Not love. Campaign contributions and strategic alliances.

"I'll be right there," I say, smoothing my skirt.

His eyes sparkle, as if to say, *Of course, you will.* Then they flick to my hand. "Beautiful ring. My wife had one similar. Though I believe yours has better clarity."

He offers his arm like we're at a cotillion, even though I gave a subtle hint that I'd follow along after he left. I place my hand on his arm because that's what Eleanor Ashby's daughter does. She performs. She pleases. She plays the game.

I rejoin the party with my spine straight and my smile fixed as Marcus slides his arm around my waist, pulling me close. "There you are," he murmurs, his lips brushing my ear. "I was beginning to think you'd escaped on a pony."

He means it as a joke, but it lands like a warning.

"The champagne," I explain, letting him think alcohol has brought the color to my cheeks. Not memories of Legion's hands. Not the phantom feel of his mouth on my pussy.

Marcus laughs, satisfied with my answer. His hand settles against the small of my back, fingers splayed possessively across silk.

If only different hands were there. Larger. Rougher. Hands with tattoos across the knuckles. Hands that have broken bones, and built fires, and traced every inch of my body in the dark.

The string quartet plays something classical and forgettable in the corner. The notes float above conversation, above laughter, above the clink of crystal against crystal.

I catch my reflection in a gilded mirror across the tent. Who is she? Would Legion even recognize me now?

Or would he only see the ghost of the girl who once climbed an old ladder in the dark just to feel alive in his arms?

The girl who kissed him with dirt on her knees and grass in her hair. The girl who sang for him when no one else was listening.

Suddenly, the crystal glasses begin to tremble on the tables, the string quartet falters, violin bows hovering mid-stroke as the musicians exchange wide-eyed glances of uncertainty.

And, as if God himself was listening to my earlier thoughts, the unmistakable thunder of motorcycles breaks the night air.

Every head turns toward the long, winding driveway, whispering…

Then the whisper swells into a primal roar that vibrates in my chest.

Familiar and terrifying all at once.

A heartbeat I thought I'd forgotten.

He's here.

He came.

CHAPTER 5
SAVANNAH

For years, I've dreamed of this rumble. I've pictured a grand entrance that comes with a grand gesture. The kind of thing that only happens in movies.

But that's all it was. A dream.

Never—*ever*—did I imagine Legion Kane might rock my world by showing up on his bike at the Ashby Ranch during my engagement party.

But he's here.

Across the tent, Colt catches my eye. My brother's lips curl into a half-smile, subtle enough that only I would notice. He raises his champagne flute slightly, a private toast between conspirators.

The gate should have been closed hours ago.

Security was Colt's responsibility. He hired ex-military men with earpieces and dark suits to patrol the perimeter. No unexpected guests. No paparazzi. *No motorcycles.*

But Colt must know me better than I thought. Because I am truly, truly surprised.

He left the gate open for Legion on purpose.

One of the security guards reaches for the radio on his shoulder, face tight with panic as the motorcycles come through the gate. Colt glides over and places a hand on the man's shoulder. He whispers something. The guard hesitates, then nods, stepping back.

My smile reaches my eyes. I love Colt.

The growl of engines builds to a roar. Not one bike. Not five. Dozens. More, I think. There's too many to count, that's for sure. So it's… the entire Badlands MC, I guess. Or somethin' very close to it. They roll onto Ashby land like a leather-clad army. Pourin' down the driveway like floodwater breaking a dam. Chrome gleaming under the fairy lights, leather cuts emblazoned with patches, faces hard as a Montana winter. The engines scream defiance against our crystal and silk, against Marcus's political ambitions, against everything this party represents.

"What the fuck?" Marcus hisses beside me, his fingers digging into my elbow.

I don't answer. Can't answer. Don't care to answer. I just keep smilin'. Oblivious, or maybe just indifferent, to the reactions all around me.

The vibrations rise up from the ground and enter my bones. A second heartbeat inside me, skippin' and stutterin' to life after years of hibernation.

The air changes instantly. The scent of expensive perfume and cologne is drowned out by gasoline and leather. The smell of real men, not these political puppets in bespoke suits.

A woman clutches her Birkin bag to her chest like it might protect her. A state senator backs into a waiter, sending a tray of tiny crab cakes crashing to the floor. Nobody stoops to clean it up. All eyes are fixed on the leather invasion drawing closer to the white tent.

Their headlights cut through the darkness like the glowing eyes of a predator.

Searching and hunting.

For me.

The bikes execute a perfect formation around the circular driveway in front of the big house. Wheels churnin' up gravel that pings against imported cars parked along the edges. Probably leaving little starburst fractures in their perfect paint jobs.

The bikers go round and round and round. Their ranks in this formation growing, swelling as more, and more bikers flow into the circle. When they are finally all here in front of us, between the house and the tent, they stop, still roaring, revving their engines.

"What do they want?" someone yells.

Marcus growls into my ear, "Yes, Savannah. What *do* they want?"

I don't answer him because I'm watching Aunt Ruth, standing frozen by the gift table, as she clutches her pearls so tightly the string snaps. White beads scatter across the wooden parquet floor like expensive hailstones, rolling under boots and heels.

No one moves to help her collect them.

Legion sits on his black Harley, no helmet, just that wild blond hair of his blowin' around his face like it's alive. His blue eyes lock with mine as we find each other across the haze of exhaust, the smell of gasoline, and the distance of years.

I don't even have to try. I could find this man in the pitch black of space.

His lips move, forming words only I can read: *You know where to find me.*

That's it. A simple six-word statement from a not-so-simple man.

I study him in a rush. Desperate to memorize everything because I know this is over. He's gonna leave any second now. So I drink him in, burning the details into my mind. He looks different. Harder, leaner, his jaw shadowed with blond stubble. New tattoos climb up his neck, disappearing beneath his collar. But his eyes—those eyes that have haunted my dreams since I was twelve—remain unchanged. The kind of blue you only find on the shore of a Caribbean beach.

Then, as suddenly as they arrived, they're leaving—a reverse avalanche of thunder and smoke. The motorcycles peel away in formation, leaving gashes in the gravel in front of the house.

The silence afterward feels unnatural, like the moment after a lightning strike before the thunder follows.

A child breaks the silence with delighted applause, quickly hushed by embarrassed parents.

Unexpectedly, I laugh. Applause, indeed.

Glasses clink as trembling hands reach for liquid courage. The string quartet tentatively resumes playing, flustered and out of time.

In the distance, the roar of engines fades like a storm moving across the valley, leaving destruction in its wake.

I exhale slowly, my chest aching with something that feels dangerously like hope.

"What. The fuck." Marcus says. His voice crackin' with rage, his campaign smile nowhere to be found. He digs his fingers deeper into my arm as he scans the empty distance. "You told me this was over," he growls. "You swore to me that it was over."

The diamond on my finger catches light as I pull away from his grip. His perfectly manicured nails leave half-moon imprints on my skin, tiny crescents of ownership.

I watch the transformation happen—the public Marcus with his Georgetown charm melting away to reveal something rawer, uglier. His jaw works beneath tanned skin, a muscle twitching with each clenched tooth. This is the face no voter will ever see on campaign posters, the face he saves for closed doors and private disappointments.

I realize with sudden clarity that I've seen this face more often than his smile lately.

Senator White materializes beside us, his voice low and urgent. "Savannah, dear, I need to know if this... display... was expected." His eyes aren't concerned— they're calculating potential donor flight. "The Nolan's are already leaving. That's forty thousand dollars walking to their car!"

The senator's cologne—sandalwood and money— overwhelms me as he leans in closer, one hand on Marcus's shoulder in warning. The elder White has perfected the art of smiling while threatening, his teeth gleaming beneath the string lights as he scans the crowd for other potential losses.

His signet ring catches the light as he gestures toward another couple edging toward the exit. "The Prestons too—that's another twenty-five. This little stunt might have just cost my son's campaign close to six figures."

He says "stunt" like others might say "murder."

Cash appears, attempting to smooth things over with the senator while Wyatt lurches close, whiskey on his breath. "You're doin' this on purpose," he hisses in my ear, swaying slightly. "You wanna keep that inheritance all to yourself. You selfish fucking bitch."

He says this as if it wasn't every one of *my* personal 'never-private' childhood moments and teenage years that made this empire what it is.

As if I *owed* him something.

As if he *deserved* something.

Wyatt's Stetson sits crooked on his head, the band dark with sweat. He's been drinking since noon—I saw the flask in his back pocket during the family photos. The brother who once taught me to ride, who carried me on his shoulders through the north pasture, now looks at me with eyes glazed by alcohol, greed, and resentment.

His fingers twist in the fabric of my blouse. Behind him, I see Cash watching, his expression calculating. Not helping, not stopping—just waiting to see which way the advantage falls.

Something snaps inside me.

I whirl on Wyatt, finger jabbing toward his chest. "Everything—the entire Eleanor Ashby photography empire, which includes this ranch—was left to *ME*. Not you. Not Cash. *ME*." My voice carries across the stunned tent. "And if you don't want me to start thinkin' about how little the two of you have done to help build this empire, you better shut the fuck up and mind your damn business."

The words hang in the air like the aftermath of gunshots. Conversations stop mid-sentence. Champagne glasses freeze halfway to parted lips. Even the waitstaff pauses, trays balanced on fingertips as they turn to watch the Ashby dynasty fracture in real time.

Wyatt's face flushes crimson beneath his tan, veins standing out on his forehead. Cash takes a step forward, then stops, eyes narrowed as he recalculates. Aunt Ruth, still clutching her broken pearl necklace, makes a small sound like a wounded bird.

I feel the weight of three hundred stares but stand taller under them, my spine straightening with each second of silence. For the first time in years, I'm not posin' for a camera—I'm standin' up for myself.

Marcus drags me away from the tent, down toward the small lake where we took our engagement photos. "I thought this was over," he shouts, his perfect hair falling across his forehead. "Was this planned? Did you know they were coming?"

Yeah, Marcus. I planned for seventy-five bikers to crash my engagement party. What fucking world do these people live in? Certainly not the one that suffocated me all through childhood. That berated me into being the perfect lady. That stole every precious moment for a photo op.

I don't even have the will to conjure up a sea of

bikers—don't even have the imagination to pull something like this off.

Because I am *broken*.

I am nothing but a shell of leftover digital pixels that lost their light a decade back.

But I don't respond. Don't even look at Marcus because the water is reflecting moonlight in ripples that remind me of motorcycle chrome.

Legion's words play on repeat in my mind: *You know where to find me.*

My wrist throbs where Marcus's fingers dig in, but the pain feels distant, unimportant. Behind us, the party continues in fragmented, awkward bursts of conversation. Someone laughs too loudly, trying to pretend nothin' has happened. A glass breaks.

Marcus is still talking—something about appearances, and donors, and how I've embarrassed him—but his words wash over me like water over stones, leaving no impression at all.

All I hear is the phantom rumble of a motorcycle engine.

All I see is the path through the cottonwoods that leads to the old grain silo, where dust motes dance in sunbeams and secrets are kept by the light of the stars.

Where Legion waits, as he always has, for me to choose.

An hour passes like a funeral. The white tent sags at the edges now, half-empty and hollowed out. Crystal champagne flutes sit abandoned on white linen, each one marked with a different shade of expensive lipstick.

Coral. Dusty rose. Blood red. Little mouth-shaped accusations left behind by women who smiled to my face, then whispered behind manicured hands about the "unfortunate interruption."

Most of the guests fled after the thunder of motorcycles faded—suddenly remembering early flights, important meetings, and sick children.

The smart ones, anyway.

The rest linger like vultures, pretendin' they're not watching me unravel thread by thread.

The waitstaff move between tables like ghosts, collecting half-eaten canapés. I hear their whispers—soft and dangerous as rattlesnakes. They've served the Ashbys for generations. They know our secrets better than we do.

"—always had a thing for that Kane boy—"

"—Eleanor would be rolling in her grave—"

"—she used to sneak out—"

Servants remember everything. Employers forget that walls have ears and champagne loosens tongues.

The string quartet packed up twenty minutes ago, their Julliard training not quite preparing them for biker invasions. Now there's just the soft electric hum of generators powering fairy lights that cast everything in a dream-like glow. Like we're all just playing pretend.

And aren't we?

Isn't that what we're doin' here? Pretendin'?

Because I never wanted this. Marcus knows I don't love him. He's a way for my brothers to get their share of the Matriarchal money.

Well, not Colt. Colt is different.

And I know that Marcus doesn't love me, either. I'm

an expedient 'partner'. That, I've learned, is what they call the wives of politicians.

How inspirin'.

He needs a wife for his campaign.

Not just any wife, but one—as he bragged earlier—with a platform that reaches over four million people and an influence in the rural demographic that is unparalleled. Love was never a plank on the campaign platform.

Senator White stands with Cash near the bar, their heads bent together in conversation that looks more like a business negotiation than small talk. Cash's face is carefully blank—the expression he wears when he's calculatin' profit margins and acceptable losses.

The Senator's mouth is a straight line, his fingers wrapped around a tumbler of bourbon so tightly I can see white knuckles from here.

Aunt Ruth sits alone at a corner table, methodically collecting pearls from her broken necklace. Each one drops into her crystal water glass with a soft 'plink' that somehow carries across the tent. Her gloves are still pristine white, despite everything.

She hasn't looked at me once since the bikers left.

I stand at the edge of the tent, one foot on grass, one on the parquet, caught between worlds like always. Marcus is ten feet away, but it might as well be ten miles.

I check my watch for the third time in ten minutes. How long will Legion wait at the silo? Is he already gone, assuming I've made my choice? Three years is a long time to hold onto hope. Even for him. Even for us. Time becomes cruel when someone you love is waiting on the other side of a choice you're afraid to make.

When I glance up, Marcus is watching me check the time, his eyes narrowing with the particular brand of suspicion that comes from wanting someone you don't trust.

I force my arm down casually, like I was just adjusting the diamond tennis bracelet he gave me for Christmas. The one that matches the ring that suddenly feels too tight on my finger.

A donor's wife approaches—Mrs. Halloway, or Hollister, or something with an H—her silk dress rustling like dry leaves as she moves.

"Such excitement earlier!" she gushes, pearls bouncing against her throat. "Was that some kind of... planned entertainment? So authentic! *So Montana!*"

I give her the Eleanor smile—lips curved just enough, eyes completely empty. Mama taught me this one before I learned to read. *It's not lying if you never actually speak the lie, Savannah Rose.*

"Just some local color," I say, the words tasting like dust in my mouth. "Montana traditions, you know."

Over her shoulder, I picture the way to the dry creek bed, It's miles from here. Miles and miles from here. But I could find my way blindfolded, that's how well I know the way.

Mrs. H-something nods like I've said something profound, then drifts away to collect more gossip for whatever charity luncheon she'll attend next week.

I move mechanically through the motions I was trained for since birth. Thanking people for coming. Accepting congratulations that feel like condolences.

Each smile costs me more than the last, like I'm spending pieces of myself I'll never get back. Each handshake is another second ticking away, another moment Legion might decide I'm not coming.

I imagine him at the silo, leaning against the weathered tin, watching the moon rise over the eastern ridge. Waiting. Patient as stone. His shoulders would be relaxed but his jaw tight—the way he always looked when he was trying not to hope for something. The image is so vivid I almost gasp out loud, earning a strange look from Wyatt's latest girlfriend.

Marcus appears at my elbow like a leash, materializing from the shadows at the edge of the tent. His fingers circle my wrist with practiced casualness—a grip that looks affectionate to observers but feels like a shackle against my pulse.

"We need to talk," he says, voice low enough that the remaining guests can't hear, but tight enough that I know it's not a request. "The library. Now."

His breath smells of expensive scotch and barely contained rage. The combination makes my skin crawl, but I nod like the well-trained Ashby girl I am. Always agreeable. Always accommodating. Always aware of watching eyes.

Except for tonight.

Eleanor really would be turning over in her grave if she heard my outburst.

But Legion's appearance wouldn't bother her.

She would've loved it.

Not him and I together, mind you.

Just *him*.

CHAPTER 6

SAVANNAH

I follow Marcus across the manicured lawn and up the stone steps to the mansion's heavy oak doors. Once through them, each step feels like a choice being made. Each footfall on marble, then hardwood, then the Persian runner that leads to the library door—all of it sounds like a countdown.

The library is filled with dark-stained wood, leather-bound books, huntin' trophies from years past, and crystal decanters filled with amber liquid that burns all the way down.

Cash's domain. A place for men. We could've had this meeting in any other room on the main floor of the mansion, but no. Marcus chooses places he feels comfortable. And this dark, masculine, testosterone-filled nod to manhood everywhere is where he's comfortable.

So ironic. Because Legion doesn't require all this pomp and he's the poster-boy for masculinity.

As Marcus closes the door behind us, the click of the

latch brings to mind images of prison cells. The room smells of polish, and privilege, and… endings.

"I can't go on like this," Marcus says, his voice crackin' as he pours himself a drink without offering me one. The amber liquid sloshes over the rim of the crystal tumbler, sticking to his fingers. "Knowing you *love* him."

The words hang between us, honest in a way we've never been. Marcus looks smaller somehow, his campaign posture collapsed under the weight of truth. For a moment, I almost feel sorry for him.

"I don't love him," I lie smoothly, the words practiced from a thousand imaginary conversations. "I don't even know him anymore." I keep my voice casual, dismissive, like we're discussing a childhood hobby I've outgrown. My fingers twist the engagement ring on my left hand, the diamond catching firelight from the chandeliers.

Marcus slams his glass down on the mahogany desk, alcohol sloshing over the rim and seeping into the wood that's older than both of us combined. "Bullshit." The word sounds foreign in his Georgetown-educated mouth, like he's trying on someone else's anger. "I saw your face when he arrived. You've never looked at me like that. Not ever." His cheeks flush with alcohol and humiliation as he runs a hand through his perfectly styled hair, messing it up in a way his campaign manager would never allow. "Not once in two years."

"You're drunk," I say, moving toward the door. I need air. I need space. I need to be anywhere but trapped in this room with the smell of scotch and desperation.

But Marcus blocks my path, his feet swaying slightly.

"Marcus, *move*." I try to step around him, but his arm shoots out, grabbing my shoulder harder than he ever has before. His fingers dig into the silk of my blouse, pressing against bone.

"Tell me the truth," he demands, voice rising to fill the cavernous room. "Just once, Savannah. Just once, be real with me."

When I try to pull away, he pushes—not hard, but enough. I stumble backward, losing my balance on the edge of the Persian rug, and fall. My palms slap against the hardwood floor, the sound echoing in the high-ceilinged room like a gunshot.

For a moment, we both freeze—me on the floor, him standing over me, his face a mask of shock at what he did. The perfect politician, the gentleman who opens doors and pulls out chairs, has been suddenly transformed into something else. Something with teeth and claws.

The library door flies open, and Colt stands there, taking in the scene with cold clarity. His normally easy smile is gone, replaced by something harder and more dangerous. Something that reminds me that we share the same blood, no matter how different we seem.

"Get out," Colt says to Marcus, his voice quiet but carrying the weight of generations of Ashby men who defend what's theirs.

"This is between me and my fiancée," Marcus protests, but his voice lacks conviction. He takes a step toward me, hand extended to help me up, but Colt moves between us, taller, with shoulders squared like he's bracing for impact.

"Not anymore," Colt says. He doesn't raise his voice, doesn't make a scene, but something in his eyes makes Marcus back up a step. "Cash is waiting to drive you back to the resort. Your father's already in the car."

The dismissal is absolute, leaving no room for argument. No negotiation. No saving face. Just the kind of swift, brutal efficiency the Ashbys are known for when someone crosses a line.

Marcus looks past Colt to where I'm still on the floor, my hair falling from its careful arrangement. "This isn't over," he says.

But we all know it is.

He turns and walks out, his expensive shoes clicking against the hardwood, the sound fading as he moves down the hallway toward the front door.

Colt helps me to my feet, his touch gentle where Marcus's was demanding. "You okay, sis?" he asks, studying my face with genuine concern. When I nod, a smile tugs at the corner of his mouth—not the polished Ashby smile for cameras, but the real one, the one we share when no one's watching.

"He's waiting for you," Colt says simply. He doesn't need to specify who. "At the silo. I saw him in Terry the other day."

My eyes crinkle up in confusion. "What do you mean you saw him in Terry? That's forty miles from here. You don't see anyone casually in Terry, Montana. Especially Legion Kane."

"Yeah, well…" Colt runs his fingers through his hair. "Another story for another time. Anyway. He told me he was gonna do this and I said I'd help. He told me to make sure you knew that he'd be waitin' for you at the silo. Even if you couldn't get away, he wanted me to tell you that."

At my surprised look, Colt shrugs, a gesture so casual it almost hides the weight of what he's saying. "What? You think you're the only one with secrets around here?" He winks, the gesture loaded with meaning and permission.

Go. Run. Live.

I hug him fiercely, breathing in the familiar scent of my brother—hay, and expensive cologne, and the faint trace of cigarettes he thinks no one knows about. "Thank you," I whisper against his shoulder.

He squeezes me once, then steps back, gesturing toward the hidden pocket doors of the library that lead to the kitchen, and a back staircase that will take me upstairs. "Better hurry," Colt says. "A man has doubts after three years inside without a word."

I blow out a breath. But just shake my head and leave.

I wanted to visit. I wanted to write. He told me absolutely not. If I came to visit, he would not accept it. If I wrote him letters, he'd sell them to other prisoners for commissary money. Which I know for a fact he would absolutely not do, but the threat was enough.

He didn't want me to visit. He didn't want me to write.

I had to respect that.

Upstairs in my bedroom, I move with quiet urgency. I strip off the designer outfit—the cream pencil skirt, the tangerine blouse hand-sewn by some woman in Paris who probably hates me, the white Lucchese boots that have never seen actual ranch work.

I shed my engagement party skin like a snake outgrowing its constraints.

From the back of my closet, behind the camera-ready clothes, I pull out a simple summer dress—pale blue cotton with a pattern of tiny white flowers, somethin' left over from more carefree years.

I wash the makeup from my face, scrubbing until my skin feels raw and real. The diamond ring catches on my washcloth, a reminder to take it off.

I place it on the vanity, where it glitters accusingly in the lamplight. Three carats. Flawless. Cold as ice against my skin, even after two weeks of wearing it.

My reflection stares back at me in the mirror—no longer the polished Ashby heiress, but someone younger, freer, with flushed cheeks and bright eyes. I look like the girl who used to climb through grain silo doors to feel alive.

I look like myself.

Then, I leave. Down the back stairs, out the back door, slidin' into shadows as the few people still here get too loud to notice a woman sneaking away in the middle of the night.

Inside the barn I relish the smell of alfalfa hay, oiled leather, and memories.

At the end stall, Cassia—my massive warmblood mare—raises her head in greeting, ears pricking forward with interest. *It's late, what are you doin' here,* those ears ask.

She nickers at me. A rumble that is so warm and real, it calms my racin' heartbeat and forces me to let out a breath. I place my hand on the side of her face, smiling. "No time for a saddle," I tell her, reaching for the bridle hanging on a hook next to her stall. Then I enter, slip the bit in her mouth and the crown over her ears. Then I lead her down the walkway, her hooves clip-clopping in the silent night.

But I don't care if anyone hears me now.

They couldn't stop me even if they did.

Once outside, I walk her over to the mounting platform, swing up onto her broad back, and grip her sides with my lower legs as she dances sideways. She knows this isn't a normal ride—there's something wild in the air tonight, something that smells like freedom.

We start at a trot, then break into a canter as we reach the first pasture. The fence looms ahead—five rails of dark wood tall enough to keep stallions in.

But Cassia was a three-star eventer back in her prime and charges forward when she sees the question I'm askin'. I lean back, feeling her gather beneath me. Powerful muscles bunching as we approach. Then we're airborne, flyin' over the fence like it's nothing but mist, landing on the other side with a soft thud.

I laugh out loud, the sound carried away by the wind as we race across the pasture, across the night, toward the silo.

Toward Legion.

Toward the only real thing I've ever wanted.

This man.

The creek bed welcomes Cassia's hooves with a symphony of crunches, each step breaking the night's silence. Moonlight catches on the cottonwoods, turning their leaves to silver coins that flutter and whisper above me. The path is exactly as I remember it—worn by water, and hooves, by two teenagers who couldn't keep their hands off each other.

If this is a dream, I'm gonna let it kill me slow.

I've been dyin' piece by piece for three years anyway—might as well go out honest.

Around the bend, the silo appears—cold, silver, still standing after all these years. It rises from the prairie like a sentinel, like it's been waiting just for me. The metal gleams under the moon, a beacon I've been avoiding and craving in equal measure.

I've made peace with a hundred things. But not this. Not him. Not the way I still get wet thinking about his mouth between my legs.

I remember, even when my mind tries to forget.

Cassia slows to a walk without me asking. She knows this place, knows what happens here. I pull her to a stop thirty yards away, suddenly unsure. The mare huffs, impatient with my hesitation.

Three years of smiling for someone else's camera.

Three years of pretending those hands didn't ruin me.

My nipples tighten against my dress. Just the memory of his touch is enough to make my body crash through every careful wall I've built. Every promise I made to forget him. To leave him behind.

And then I see him.

Legion leans in the open silo door like he never left, like time stopped the day they locked him away. He's a shadow against warm golden light inside. The moonlight catches on his face, illuminating cheekbones that look sharper now, a jaw that's set harder. The last traces of boyhood gone from his features. Like life has carved away everything soft and only pure longing remains. I can see it in how he stands—like he's deciding whether to worship me, or destroy me, or both.

When his eyes find mine, wet heat pools between my legs. That gaze of his is hungry. Patient, but predatory. His eyes track my every movement, missing nothing.

Cassia shifts under me, sensing my tension. My fingers shake on the reins, betraying my careful composure. My heart hammers against my ribs like it's trying to escape, trying to reach him before the rest of me can.

I'm soaked through my panties and he hasn't even touched me yet. Hasn't said a word. Just stands there, watching me with those eyes that have always seen right through me.

He steps away from the golden light behind him, entering the dark shadows. Moonlight filters down through cottonwood leaves, making him sparkle a bit. When he's close enough that I can smell him—leather, and smoke, and something darker—he reaches out his hand.

Just his hand, palm up. Nothing more.

It's an invitation. Not to love him, or be with him, just to fuck him.

That's all these silo visits have ever been. Friendship and fucking. Because even as children—before the sex, obviously—we knew we didn't belong in the real world. We existed only as something provisional and transitory.

He invited me here for sex. And I could lie. Say I didn't come here for that. But that's all it is, just a lie.

Neither of us says a word as I place my hand in his and the moment our skin connects, electricity shoots straight to my core. A small sound escapes my throat—not quite a gasp, not quite a moan. Something in between that I'd be embarrassed by if anyone else heard it.

Legion helps me down slow, hands warm on my waist. The strength in them is familiar and foreign all at once—the same hands, but harder now. More certain.

My feet hit the ground and I break open.

I've been good for too long. Polite. Clean. Untouched. Marcus kisses me like I'm made of glass. Legion fucks me like I'm made of fire.

My legs are unsteady beneath me. I am crumbling with one touch.

His hands linger at my waist, thumbs brushing against the thin fabric of my dress.

"Savannah," he says, and my name in his mouth sounds like a prayer, and a curse, and a blessing all wrapped up into one.

Then his lips meet mine and it's not sweet—it's desperate.

It's the kiss you give someone after three years of silence.

After too many nights with the wrong name on your tongue.

This isn't romance. This is possession. This is me

handing over everything I tried to bury. He tastes like salvation and sin, and I wanna *drown* in it.

I moan into his mouth, shameless and hungry. My hips press against his thigh and I can feel how hard he already is. His hands tangle in my hair, pulling just enough to make me gasp.

He breaks the kiss, both of us breathing hard. "Inside," he says, voice rough with want.

He leads me through the silo door, and I'm not prepared for what I see. Fairy lights strung across the metal walls cast a soft glow over the space.

Blankets—actual clean blankets—spread across the dirt floor.

Sage bundles hanging from the rafters.

Wildflowers in mason jars.

He built this while I was pretendin' to be the perfect future wife. That's all I've ever done at home. Just pretendin'.

But everything with Legion is real.

This is the place where he takes me apart.

It's also the place where he puts me back together.

My pussy clenches with anticipation. I'm already imagining his mouth between my legs, his hands holding my knees apart while I come against the thrusting of his tongue.

"When did you do this?" I ask, gesturing to the space around us.

"This afternoon," he says, eyes never leaving mine. "Finished it right before we paid our respects to your future husband."

I don't say anything back to that last bit—but he's not waiting for it anyway.

He knows who I belong to.

Him.

He knew I'd come.

I reach for the hem of my dress, pulling it over my head. The night air kisses my naked skin, raising goosebumps across my bare nipples. Legion watches, unmoving, as I slip my panties down my legs and stand before him like an offering.

There was never any doubt we were gonna fuck.

It's all we do.

We never dated. We never went dancin' and drinkin'.

We just fuck. And when we fuck, we fuck hard.

Legion's eyes roam over me, taking in every inch, every change the years have wrought. His shirt comes off. The angel and the demon inked into his chest staring back at me now. New tattoos, prison tattoos, covering scars I don't remember.

I understand exactly who he is in this moment—a man caught between salvation and damnation, fighting both as hard as he can. He fights what he is harder than any man I've ever known.

And still he holds space for me inside all that rage

"I've been empty without you," I whisper, the words torn from somewhere deep inside me. "Show me I'm still yours. Make me remember what it feels like to be claimed."

And then he's here. Hands cupping my face with a gentleness that belies the hunger in his eyes. His thumbs trace my cheekbones, my lips, the line of my jaw. His touch is reverent. Mapping my body like he's memorizing scripture.

Every scar, every freckle, every place that makes me gasp.

"You're so fucking beautiful it hurts to look at you," he growls against my throat, and I wanna tell him I've been ugly without him. Performing pretty instead of feeling it.

His mouth trails down my neck, across my collarbone, leaving fire in its wake. When he reaches my breast, his tongue circles my nipple before taking it between his teeth. I arch against him, a sound between a whimper and a moan escaping my lips.

His hands slide down my sides, gripping my hips, my ass, pulling me against him so I can feel how hard he is through his jeans. I reach between us, palming him through the denim, and he hisses through his teeth.

"I tried to forget," I gasp as his fingers trail lower, tracing the inside of my thigh. "Tried to want someone else."

It's a lie.

I didn't try at all.

There is no one else for me but the man standing right here with his hand between my legs.

Legion's fingers find me wet and ready, and the sound he makes is almost pained. "Fuck, Savannah," he mutters, sliding one finger inside me, then another. His thumb circles my clit, and my hips buck against his hand.

I fumble with his belt, desperate to feel him, all of him. He helps me, kicking off his boots, jeans, and boxers until he's naked against me, hard length pressed against my stomach.

We sink to the blankets together, a tangle of limbs

and need. He positions himself between my thighs, the head of his cock teasing my entrance. Our eyes meet, and in that moment, everything else falls away but us.

When he slides inside me, we both go still.

This is home.

This is church.

This is the religion they'll damn us both for practicing.

He begins to move, slow and deep and devastating. Each thrust brings me closer to the edge, closer to the truth I've been running from.

This is when reality hits.

This is when I understand the choice I'm really making.

I'm gonna lose everything—my family, my inheritance, my carefully constructed life.

But I don't care.

At least, not right now.

I just come apart in his arms, moaning his name as his endless battle between good and evil plays out across his chest in ink that reminds us both that this love we have… is *forbidden*.

CHAPTER 7
LEGION

Angels sound like salvation you don't deserve.

Demons feel like the damnation you've earned.

Savannah tastes like both.

Her body arches beneath me, lips parted, eyes half-closed. The fairy lights I strung up this afternoon catch in her hair, making her glow while she falls apart. I hold back, grinding my teeth against the need to follow her over. Not yet. I wanna watch her first.

Wanna see if she still looks the same when she comes. If she still whispers my name like it's something holy instead of the curse it is.

She does.

Three years locked away, and her body still remembers mine. Still responds to my fingers, my mouth, my cock like we were made to fit together. Like we didn't spend a thousand nights apart.

I pull out and she reaches for me, grabbing at my cock to put it back inside her. But I shake my head. "I'm gonna go slow now. I needed to be inside you, but now I want to go slow.

I trace my fingertips over her nipples, feeling them harden under my touch. Trail down her ribs, counting each one. She's thinner than before. Sharper. Like prison carved parts of her away too.

My hand slides over her hip, stopping at the small tattoo there. Seven words inked into her skin:

A place where damnation and light begin.

The last line of a poem I wrote her when we were sixteen. When I was still stupid enough to believe words could capture what we were to each other. Because that's where we live. That's where we've always lived. In some unholy purgatory where love is evil.

"You kept it," I murmur, running my thumb over the ink.

She nods, breath still coming fast. "It's the only part of you they can't ever take from me."

I don't tell her I recited that poem every night in my cell. Line by line. Word by word. Like a prayer or a curse or both.

I slide down her body, spreading her thighs. She's wet and swollen, and when I put my mouth on her, she makes a sound that would bring angels to their knees.

I work her with my tongue, with my fingers, until she's shaking again. Until she's gripping my hair so hard it hurts. Until she's coming against my mouth, my name a broken plea on her lips.

This is what we are. What we've always been. Fire and ruin. Grace and sin. *Forbidden longings burning from within.*

I kiss my way back up her body, tasting salt and sweetness. When I reach her mouth, I kiss her deep, letting her taste herself on my tongue.

"Turn over," I tell her, voice rough with need.

She doesn't hesitate. Doesn't question. Just rolls onto her stomach, face pressed into the blankets, ass raised slightly. Waiting.

I spread her legs wider, positioning myself between them. Run my hands over the curve of her spine, the swell of her ass. She shivers under my touch.

"Look at me," I say, and she turns her head, eyes meeting mine over her shoulder.

I push into her slow, watching her face as I fill her. The way her lips part. The way her eyes flutter closed. The way she bites down on her bottom lip to keep from crying out.

"Don't," I growl, reaching around to grip her jaw. "I wanna hear you."

She nods, and when I thrust deeper, she moans my name. Loud enough to echo off the silo walls. Loud enough for God himself to hear.

I fuck her hard and deep, one hand gripping her hip, the other tangled in her hair. Each thrust pushes us both closer to the edge. Each sound she makes strips away another layer of prison-hardened skin.

"Mine," I mutter against her shoulder, teeth grazing the soft flesh there. "Always been mine."

"Yes," she gasps, pushing back against me. "Yours."

I believe her. Even though she wears another man's ring—it's missing now, but the shadow of it remains, burned into her skin like a brand on a bull.

Even though she built a life without me. In this

moment, with my cock buried inside her and her body trembling beneath mine, she's *mine*.

This wasteland keeps their secret, dark and grim.

When I feel her tightening around me again, I let go. Let the heat and pressure build until there's nothing left but release. I come inside her with a groan that starts somewhere in my chest, emptying myself into the only woman who's ever seen past the ink, and the scars, and the rage.

A place where damnation and light begin.

I don't pull out right away. Just collapse on top of her, careful to keep most of my weight on my forearms. Her skin is slick with sweat, her heart hammering against her ribs. I press my lips to the back of her neck, tasting salt.

"I'm gonna ruin you," I whisper, and it's not a threat.

It's a warning. A promise. A confession.

She reaches back, fingers finding mine, squeezing tight. "I've been waiting three years to be ruined."

I roll onto my back, pulling Savannah against me. Her skin sticks to mine, sweat cooling between us. The silo creaks and groans—metal shifting in the restless prairie wind.

Or maybe it's ghosts. Same damn thing in Montana. The dead don't rest here; they just find different ways to haunt you.

"You're quiet," she whispers, fingers tracing the new scars on my chest. Prison souvenirs. Her touch is feather-light, as if she's reading braille, trying to decipher the story written in my skin.

I don't answer. Nothing to say that doesn't taste like regrets. My words turn to dust before they reach my tongue.

This was never gonna work.

Not then. Not now. Not ever.

Has nothing to do with how my heart pounds like a war drum when she's near or how my hands still remember every curve of her body.

Has everything to do with blood, and dirt, and concrete. The walls between our worlds built higher than any prison fence I could ever climb.

She's Savannah fucking Ashby. Instagram royalty. Montana aristocracy. Woman with a future bright enough to blind.

I'm the man whose name means "many."

Many demons.

Many sins.

Many scars.

Many reasons this ends bloody.

Just another Kane marked for destruction, carrying curses instead of promises.

The fairy lights I hung earlier flicker against the metal walls, casting honey-gold shadows across her bare shoulders. Three hours of work for this moment. This beautiful lie. This last time.

Climbing rickety ladders, stringing delicate bulbs with calloused hands that have broken men's jaws. Playing at tenderness when we both know what I am.

"What are you thinking about?" she asks, voice heavy with sleep, eyelids fluttering. Always could fall asleep anywhere. In this rusted silo. In my beat-up truck. Against my shoulder while I drove her home before dawn, back when we were kids playing at rebellion, stealing moments between sunset and sunrise, thinking we were invincible.

I never sleep when she's with me. Too busy memorizing. Cataloging. Storing up for the winter that's always coming. The curve of her hip. The freckle behind her ear. The way her breath catches when I touch her just right.

It's all ammunition against loneliness.

"You're allowed to marry him," I say, the words scraping my throat raw, tasting of surrender.

She laughs, soft and sleepy against my chest. Doesn't even open her eyes, just nuzzles closer like a cat seeking warmth. "Since when do I need your permission, Legion?"

Since always. She knows it. I know it. The dirt knows it. The ghosts in this silo know it. The scars on my knuckles spelling my sister's name know it.

We all know it.

"I mean it," I say, voice harder now. "You should marry him. White House Marcus with his clean hands and Georgetown degree."

Now she looks up, those blue eyes narrowing, sleep vanishing like mist under a harsh sun. "What are you talking about?"

I sit up, dislodging her from my chest, reaching for my jeans crumpled on the floor. My shirt. My boots. All the armor I dropped when she rode in on her hundred-thousand-dollar horse, hair wild, eyes wilder. "You need to get back before they miss you. Before someone comes looking."

"Legion—" My name on her lips still sounds like prayer, even after everything.

"They're gonna notice." I pull my shirt over my head, covering the ink, the scars, the places her fingers just touched. "The Little Ashby Princess can't disappear at her own engagement party. Not with half the state's political machine watching."

She sits up, blanket clutched to her chest like virtue she abandoned hours ago. "Don't call me that."

I don't answer. Just finish lacing my boots with quick, efficient movements. Stand up. Offer her my hand. "You need to go."

For a second, she doesn't move. Just stares at me, something breaking behind those eyes—oceans freezing over in real time. Then she takes my hand, lets me pull her to her feet, our bodies close enough that I can feel her heart hammering against mine.

She dresses silently, efficiently. No more words between us. Just the sound of fabric against skin. The rustle of her fixing her hair, erasing the evidence of my fingers tangled in golden strands.

The heartbreak isn't that she's leaving. It's that she believes me when I push her away - as if there was ever a universe where I didn't want her to stay, as if I could ever mean the words that cut between us like barbed wire.

I knew this day was coming. Even before prison swallowed three years of my life. Even before I let her go the first time. Some things are written in blood, not ink. Some fates are carved in bone before you're born.

"That worlds will shake if they should truly touch," I say, quoting the poem she tattooed on her ribs.

She finishes straightening her dress, smoothing expensive fabric over hips I just held, then steps close. Places her hands on my face, thumbs brushing over stubble. Kisses me once, soft and final, tasting of goodbye and broken promises.

"It has only ever been you," she whispers against my mouth, breath mingling with mine one last time.

Then she's gone, stepping out of the silo into the moonlight, whistling for her horse with two fingers between perfect lips. I watch through the doorway as she mounts up, bareback and barefoot, and rides away across the silver-washed prairie.

Back to her mansion.

Her fiancé.

Her life.

Her destiny that never included a man named Legion.

I stand in the empty silo, fairy lights might as well be prison bars. The ghost of her perfume lingers, mixing with dust and memory.

This is the end. I swear it.

It's over.

I just needed to see her one last time.

And now I'll set her free.

CHAPTER 8

LEGION

The desert out past Terry isn't just pretty, it's honest. Scarred earth that doesn't pretend to be anything but what it is—broken ground that'll break you back if you aren't careful.

Been that way since before names.

Will be that way long after they're gone.

Unforgiving and relentless, like the sun that beats down on it day after day, turning everything to dust and memory. The kind of place that strips a man down to his bones and leaves him raw.

The sky bleeds pink at the edges when I hit the dirt road leading to the clubhouse. Forty minutes of hard riding from the silo, dust coating my throat, Savannah's scent still clinging to my skin beneath leather and sweat.

Each mile puts distance between what I want and what I get.

The taste of her lingers on my lips, a ghost I can't

exorcise, while the rumble of my bike beneath me reminds me where I belong.

Two worlds.

No bridge between them.

Just a chasm filled with broken promises and things we never said out loud.

My headlight cuts through dawn shadows as I round the final bend, and immediately, I know—somethin's wrong.

The gates are wide open at Clubhouse. No prospects hangin' around. No guards. Just emptiness where security should be.

The protocol's clear—gates stay locked. Always. Even if they saw me coming on the cameras hidden in the rocks, someone should be posted. Always two men minimum.

That's how we've survived this long.

That's how we keep the law, rivals, and ghosts at bay.

I slow the bike, engine growling low as I roll through.

There's no movement as I scan the perimeter, just the hulking shape of the clubhouse against the lightening sky, windows dark, parking lot filled with familiar bikes.

Diesel's chopper. Roach's custom seat. Brick's immaculate Street Glide.

All present, all silent.

The collection of steel and chrome gleams dully in the half-light, machines at rest while their riders are nowhere to be seen.

The skin between my shoulder blades tightens as I park next to Diesel's chopper and kill the engine.

The silence is wrong. There's no music no voices, no sounds of life. Just the cooling tick of my engine. And I get it, it's early. But this place is never silent.

The clubhouse stands like a fortress in front me. A place with secrets, that's for sure. But this isn't that kind of secret. I dismount, boots crunching on the gravel, and leave my helmet hanging on the handlebar.

The clubhouse door stands half-open. Another broken rule. Nothing about this feels right. I approach slow, shoulders squared, weight balanced on the balls of my feet. The angels inked across my back seem to tense with me, their tattooed wings spreading across muscle, the celestial war etched into my skin readying for battle.

When I step inside, the place explodes. The slow toll of a bell rings out, deep and deliberate, echoing through the walls just before the guitar kicks in—AC/DC's *"Hell's Bells"* cranked so loud the floorboards shake under my boots. Then the lights slam on, flooding the room with harsh fluorescence that burns my eyes. The assault is total —sound, light, memory—like the first moment out of solitary, when everything's too bright, too loud, too much.

"DEMON'S HOME!" Diesel's voice booms over the chaos, his six-foot-five frame materializing from the crowd. Arms wide, beard wild, gold tooth catching the light as he grins. "The fucking legend returns!" His massive shoulders block out the light behind him, casting his face in shadow except for that gleaming tooth and the glint in his eyes.

I blink, frozen in the doorway. Every patched member stands in formation—a circle of leather and denim, faces I know better than my own reflection. Men I've fought with, bled with, hell, probably shouldn't admit this, but... killed for.

They're all holding whiskey or beer raised high above their heads. Eyes hungry with something that looks like respect but borders on reverence. The air thick with cigarette smoke, whiskey fumes, and anticipation.

The worn leather couch where prospects sleep is shoved against the wall, springs visible through torn upholstery. The church table—hand-carved oak that's witnessed twenty years of club business, knife marks and cigarette burns telling stories no one speaks aloud —is covered in bottles, glasses, and lines of powder nobody bothers hiding. The walls around us bear witness, covered in photos of brothers living and dead, territory maps marked with red pins, patches taken from enemies who didn't survive the encounter.

I don't move. Don't speak. Just breathe in the familiar smell of cigarettes and brotherhood. The scent of men who live outside laws but inside codes stronger than prison bars. Men who understand loyalty isn't about words—it's about silence when it matters most.

Brick steps forward from the circle. Club president since before I could ride. Face like weathered stone, eyes that miss nothing. He's holding something in his hands—a leather cut, new and unmarked except for the center patch. The Badlands insignia. Skull wrapped in barbed wire, rising from cracked earth. The colors I've earned in blood and silence. The same symbol that marks the clubhouse walls, the bikes outside, the flesh of every man in this room.

"Three years," Brick says, voice carrying even over the pounding music. "Three years you kept your mouth shut. Carried our weight. Walked in a prospect, walking out a brother." His words hang in the air, heavy with meaning only we understand. "There were times, Demon, when I didn't think you'd make it. Hell, no man I've ever known has been around so damn long and taken so damn long to earn his fuckin' patch."

I blow out a breath. Not wanting to think about that.

"But you showed up. You came through," Brick adds.

The unspoken truth: I took the fall. I did the time. I kept the code.

The room erupts again. Boots pound against the floor in unison—a rhythm that the blues blaring form the juke—an earthquake in my head.

War drums. Heartbeat.

Blood rushing before a fight.

The sound reverberates through my chest, replacing the hollow space where Savannah's name used to echo. The vibration travels up through my legs, settles in my bones like a second pulse.

I still don't move. Something's happening here that I stopped expecting that day Cash got me out early.

Something sacred and dangerous.

Something that smells like fire and eternity.

The air crackles with it, electric and alive.

Chains steps up beside Brick, tattooed hands cradling two objects. A blowtorch and an iron rod with its end shaped into a crude letter 'B'.

His glass eye catches the light, reflecting nothing while his good eye gleams with anticipation. The intricate designs covering his fingers—prison work, done with guitar string and ballpoint ink—dance as he adjusts his grip on the torch.

"Going old school tonight," Chains says, voice rough from years of smoke and shouting. "Won't just wear the patch. You'll become it." His words carry weight beyond their sound, an ancient promise passed from brother to brother since before the club had a name.

The torch ignites with a hiss. Blue flame licks at metal until it glows red-hot, casting an unholy light across the circle of watching faces. The brand pulses with heat, hungry for flesh. The metal seems alive in Chains' hands, a living thing with its own purpose and will.

Silence falls. Even the music seems to dim, as if the speakers themselves know to respect what's coming. The only sound is the soft roar of the torch and the collective breathing of men who understand what this moment means.

This isn't standard. This is reserved for the ones who've bled. The ones who've killed. The ones who've done time. The ones who've proven loyalty beyond question or doubt. The sacred ritual that transforms a member into a legend.

I understand now.

Not just a patch party.

Initiation. Rebirth. Branding.

Roach appears at my side, twitchy hands steady for once as he presses a bottle of whiskey into my hand. "Drink deep, brother. Then we make it official." His eyes dart around, always calculating, always watching for threats, but tonight they're focused only on me. For once, his paranoia is at rest, replaced by something like reverence.

I take the bottle. Tilt it back. Let burn wash away Savannah's taste still lingering on my tongue. Amber liquid spills down my chin, soaks my shirt. No one laughs. They watch with reverence. With hunger. With the look of men who've passed through this fire and emerged transformed. The whiskey burns a trail down my throat, settles in my empty stomach like liquid courage.

When I lower the bottle, Diesel's there. Hunting knife glinting as he cuts away my shirt, exposing skin over my heart. There's a demon there already, but not for long.

The blade is sharp enough that I barely notice it slice through fabric, just the cool air hitting newly exposed skin.

Brick holds out the cut. "Family forever. Blood in, blood out." His voice carries the weight of twenty years of leadership, of decisions that have built and protected this brotherhood through war and peace.

I look around the room. Faces of men who would kill for me.

Lie for me.

Die for me.

Men nothing like me and everything like me at the same time.

Crow stands silent against the wall, eyes watchful beneath his dark brows. Some prospect watching with hungry eyes, desperate to earn what I'm being given.

Butch with his scarred knuckles wrapped around a bottle, nodding with respect. Each man bearing his own scars, visible and hidden, each one bound by the same code that brought me here.

Not one looks away. Not one flinches as Chains approaches with the glowing brand. The air fills with the smell of heated metal and anticipation, thick enough to choke on.

For the first time since walking out of prison, something like belonging settles in my bones.

Tastes like home. Not the home I dreamed of inside.

Not the home with Savannah's laugh echoing through clean rooms.

But a home nonetheless.

A place where my demons are welcome, where my silence is understood, where my loyalty is rewarded.

I nod once. Sharp and decisive.

Ready for the mark.

Ready to become what I've already been for years.

Ready to make official what prison and pain have already carved into my soul.

Chains presses the iron against my chest.

White-hot agony tears through me. The smell of my own burning flesh fills my nostrils, choking me worse than any prison smoke. I don't make a sound. I've learned to swallow pain. Learned to let it sink into bone rather than spill from my mouth.

The club roars around me—thunder in human form. Their voices blur into a single, primal sound. Not cheering. Something older. Something sacred.

The iron lifts away. The pain doesn't. It pulses with each heartbeat, angry and alive.

Diesel steps forward, slaps a bandage over raw, branded skin. "Wear it proud," he says, voice low enough that only I hear. "You earned it twice."

Brick holds out the cut again. Black leather, worn soft at the edges. Badlands MC patch sewn into the back—skull wrapped in barbed wire, rising from cracked earth.

The symbol of what we are. What I am now.

I slide my arms through. The weight settles on my shoulders like judgment. Like belonging.

"To Legion," Brick calls, raising his glass. "Blood in."

"Blood in," the room echoes.

The celebration becomes a blur after that. Whiskey flows. Music pounds. Stories spill—prison tales, run stories, near-misses with death.

I drink until the burn in my chest becomes background noise.

Until Savannah's ghost stops haunting the corners of my vision.

Two hours later, I drag myself up the metal stairs to the bunkhouse. Each step echoes, bouncing off concrete walls. My new brand throbs beneath the bandage, a heartbeat of fire just left of center. The cut hangs heavy on my shoulders, still stiff with newness.

My head swims with whiskey. Too much. Not enough. The kind of drunk where the room tilts but memories still cut clear. Where you remember everything you're trying to forget.

The upstairs hallway stretches longer than it should. Doors line both sides—some open to empty rooms, some closed tight. I count them as I pass. Habit from inside. Always know your exits. Always count your steps.

Room 3. Mine now. Has been since I got out, technically, but tonight makes it real. Tonight makes everything real.

I shoulder the door open. Don't bother with the light switch. Sunlight spills through the duct-taped window, casting golden light across the sparse furnishings. Steel-frame bed against one wall. Gun rack, empty except for the 12-gauge I keep for emergencies. Metal locker for clothes. Door in the corner leading to a tiny bathroom—the only room in this hallway with an en suite.

My smile is stupid, but it's real.

I made it.

I fuckin' made it.

Nah, it's not the home I hoped for. But it is still a home. Which is more than I can say for that godforsaken trailer that spits out evil every time someone goes in.

I'm halfway to the bed when I see her.

Small shape curled on my mattress. Dark hair spilling across my pillow. Knees tucked to chest.

Mercy.

Fuck.

I forgot she was here.

She's fast asleep, wearing someone's borrowed shorts and a club t-shirt that ten sizes too big for her. She's got the BB gun tucked against her chest like a teddy bear, finger resting near the trigger even in sleep. Her face is relaxed in a way it never is when she's awake—softer, younger. Reminds me how fucking young nine really is.

I stand there swaying, trying to decide what to do. My drunk brain offers no solutions. I should sleep on the floor. Let her have the bed. But my body aches for a tiny bit of comfort as the brand throbs under my cut.

"Mercy," I whisper, then realize I'm still too loud. Prison voice. She doesn't stir. Sleeps the deep sleep of the exhausted, the kind I haven't had since before Whitefall.

I ease down onto the edge of the bed, careful not to disturb her. The mattress dips under my weight. Springs creak in protest.

Her eyes snap open. Alert instantly. No slow drift to consciousness. One moment asleep, the next fully aware, gun barrel shifting to center on my chest.

"Easy, there," I slur. "Juss me."

Recognition dawns. The gun lowers fractionally.

"You smell like whiskey," she says, voice scratchy with sleep.

"Yeahhhhh." No point denying it. "Party got wild. You okay up here alone?"

She nods, sitting up. The BB gun never leaves her grip. "Diesel brought me food. Said to wait for you."

"You can have the bed," I tell her, starting to stand. "I'll take the—"

"No." Her hand shoots out, grabbing my wrist. Surprising strength in those small fingers. "Stay."

I look down at her. Really look. See the fear hiding behind those Kane eyes—the same eyes that stare back at me from the mirror. Fear of being left. Of being alone. Of waking up and finding everyone gone again.

"Ight," I say, kicking off my boots. I'm hardly in the mood to put up a fight. Especially over something I want. "Scoot over."

She slides to the wall, making room. I stretch out beside her, on top of the thin blanket while she stays beneath it. The bed's barely big enough for me, let alone both of us, but we make it work. She curls against my side, small and warm, the BB gun now pointed safely away.

"They burned you," she says, not a question. Her eyes fixed on the bandage visible through my torn shirt.

"Yeahhhhh."

"Does it hurt?"

"Yeahhhhh."

"Good," she says with fierce satisfaction. "Means it's real."

I chuckle with my eyes closed. Smart kid. Too smart. Sees right through me, right through everything. Always has.

"What's it mean?" she asks after a minute. "The mark."

I open my eyes and stare at the ceiling, watching shadows dance across water stains. "Means I belong here now. Means they belong to me."

"Like family?"

"Somethin' like that."

She's quiet for so long I think she's fallen back asleep. Then her small voice drifts up again. "Will they help us find Destiny?"

The question hits. Destiny. My middle sister. Seventeen, and pregnant, and gone.

Another failure. Another person I couldn't protect.

"Yeahhhhh," I promise, though I have no right to. "They will."

"The demons will help?" she asks, and there's something in her voice—not fear, but something close to reverence.

I look down at her. "Whah?"

"At school," she says, matter-of-fact, "they call you Demon Kane. Say you got demons inside you. A whole legion of them."

A laugh bubbles up from somewhere deep, somewhere I thought had dried up years ago. "That what they say?"

She nods solemnly. "Miss Wilkins tried to make them stop. Said it wasn't nice. But Tommy Harkinson said his dad told him it's true. Said Mark 5:9 proves it."

Mark 5:9.

The verse that gave me my name.

The curse my mother spoke over me the day I was born, high on something that made her see angels and demons battling for her soul.

"My name is Legion," I whisper, "for we are many."

Mercy's eyes widen. "So it *is* true?"

I should tell her no. Should explain it's just a story, just people being cruel. Should protect her from the weight of our family's reputation.

Instead, I say, "Maybe it is. Maybe I do have demons inside me." I brush hair from her forehead, gentler than I knew I could be. "But they're my demons, Merce. And they'll tear apart anyone who tries to hurt you."

She considers this, head tilted like she's working through a complex math problem. Then she nods, satisfied with my answer. "Good." She settles back against me, eyes drifting closed. "I like having a demon for a brother."

Within minutes, her breathing evens out. Sleep reclaims her, innocent and deep.

I lie awake, staring at the ceiling, feeling the brand pulse on my chest and my sister's small body curled trustingly against mine.

My demons and I, we'll keep watch.

CHAPTER 9
LEGION

The dream starts the same way it always does—with fire.

I'm standing on a battlefield of bones. The sky is split open like a wound, oozing crimson light and the air tastes like blood.

Across from me stands... *me*.

But not me.

My face on an angel's body, wings spread wide, flaming sword raised. His eyes burn with righteous fury, but his mouth twists with doubt.

Opposite him stands another me—demon-faced, horned, fanged, scarred. Laughing. Always laughing.

"My name is Legion," the angel-me whispers.

"For we are many," the demon-me finishes.

They circle each other, these twin versions of myself, neither fully winning, neither fully dyin'. I try to scream, try to move, but I'm frozen between them.

For some reason, I'm not participatin' in this battle. I'm just a witness.

Blood begins risin' up from the ground. Droplets formin', defyin' gravity, floating up like rain in reverse. It beads on my skin, then pulls away, drawn to the sky.

The angel-me turns, fixing me with eyes that burn. "You *chose* this," he says, my mother's voice coming from its mouth. "You chose this the day you were born."

The demon laughs, the sound shattering the air like glass. "Tell him the truth," it growls. "Tell him what happens when the blood reaches the sky."

I look up. The blood droplets converge, forming a perfect circle. A clock face. A countdown.

"My name is Legion," I try to say.

"For we are many," every voice I've ever known answers back.

The blood-clock strikes thirteen—

BANG BANG BANG

I jerk awake, hand already reaching for the shank under my pillow that's not there. Heart hammering against my ribs. Sweat-soaked sheets twisted around my legs.

"Kane! Wake the fuck up!" Roach's voice cuts through the door. "Brick wants you. *Now*."

I blink at the ceiling, dragging myself back to reality. The clubhouse. My bunk. The morning after patching in.

The space beside me is empty. Mercy's gone.

"Two minutes," I groan back, voice rough with sleep.

"Make it one," Roach answers, footsteps already retreating down the hall.

I swing my legs over the edge of the bed, wincing as the movement pulls at the fresh brand on my chest. The bandage Diesel applied last night is spotted with blood and clear fluid. I peel it back carefully, hissing through my teeth.

The Badlands B stares back at me, angry, red, and black. The skin around it swollen and weeping. It's not just a mark, it's a covenant. Permanent and binding.

No goin' back now.

Not that there ever was a goin' back.

I stand, stretching my stiff muscles until they ache. The dream clings to me like smoke, that reversed blood rain still vivid behind my eyelids.

"Why me?" I mumble to the remnants of the dream. "Why do they haunt *me*? It's just a name, for fuck's sake."

The shower is a brutal awakening. Water pressure too high, temperature swinging between scalding and freezing. The spray hits my chest and the pain is immediate and electric. I grit my teeth against it, letting it wash over me.

When I get out I realize that someone left a tube of aloe gel on the edge of the sink, alongside a white pill I recognize as oxy. Thoughtful.

I take the aloe but put the oxy inside the medicine cabinet along with a whole line of pills people been tryin' to give me since I got here four days ago. I need my head clear for whatever Brick wants.

I dress in clean jeans but no shirt. Not today, Satan. Can't even stand the thought of fabric against the raw flesh of my brand. I can't even wear the cut. It'll have to wait.

Downstairs, the clubhouse is quiet. Morning-after kind of quiet. The kind that comes with hangovers and regrets. Crow sits at the bar, methodically cleaning a .45, piece by piece. He nods at me but doesn't speak.

"Mercy?" I ask.

He jerks his head toward the back door. "Range."

I step outside into the harsh Montana morning. The sun's barely up, but the air already carries that dry heat that promises a scorcher by noon. The sound of gunfire draws me around the side of the building to the shooting range. It's just a dirt berm backstop and target frames made of repurposed metal signs, but it gets the job done.

Diesel stands behind Mercy, his massive hands adjusting her grip on a rifle that looks too big for her small frame. She squints down the sight, face set in concentration.

"Breathe out and squeeze," Diesel instructs. "Don't pull."

She does. The rifle cracks. A sign fifty yards away pings and stutters.

"Good girl," Diesel says, pride evident. "Natural. Just like your brother."

Something twists in my gut watching this. My nine-year-old sister learning to shoot from an outlaw biker. There's a wrongness to it. But there's a rightness too. This world doesn't spare children. Better she knows how to defend herself than end up dead because she can't.

"Mornin'," I call.

Mercy turns, face lighting up when she sees me. Then carefully lowers the rifle, barrel down, finger off the trigger. At least Diesel's teaching her right.

"I hit five in a row," she says, pride making her stand taller.

"That's my girl," I say, and mean it. "Gotta see Brick. You good here?"

She nods, already turning back to her lesson. Diesel gives me a solemn nod. Message received. He'll watch her.

Brick's office sits at the back of the clubhouse, separated from the main room by a heavy wooden door. I knock twice, wait for his gruff "Enter," then step inside.

First time I've been in here since my release. Not much has changed. Same scarred desk. Same maps on the walls, marked with routes only Brick understands. Same smell of cigar smoke and old leather.

Brick himself sits behind the desk, phone pressed to his ear, as he stares at the floor. He's a big man, tall and solid, with the kind of face that's weathered rather than aged. Gray in his beard, none in his resolve.

"Don't care what they said," he's saying into the phone. "Price is the price. Border's hot right now... Yeah, well, that's not my fucking problem, is it?" He glances up, sees me, and gestures for me to sit. "Look, I gotta go. Have it there by Friday or the deal's off." He hangs up without waiting for a response.

I take the offered seat, trying not to look too obvious as I look around and take stock of the place. Filing cabinets against the wall, safe bolted to the floor, stack of burner phones on the corner of the desk. This room holds the secrets that sent me to prison. The secrets I kept.

"How's the brand?" Brick asks, lighting a cigar.

"Hurts."

He nods, approving. "Good. Should hurt. Means something that way." He studies me, eyes giving nothing away. "The kid can't stay here."

It's not what I expected him to say. I tense. "Mercy? She's not—"

"Relax." He raises a hand. "Not saying she can't be around. Just can't live here. The clubhouse isn't a place for a kid. Especially not a girl."

He reaches into a drawer, pulls out a manila envelope, and slides it across the desk. "Open it."

I do. Inside is cash—a lot of it. Twenty grand, maybe more. And papers. Legal papers. I spread them out, trying to make sense of what I'm seeing. Title deed. Insurance forms. Utility particulars.

"What is this?" I ask, though I'm starting to understand.

"Your place," Brick says simply. "Double-wide. Three bedrooms."

I stare at him, then back at the papers. "I don't understand."

"Brotherhood means something here," Brick says, leaning forward. "It's not just ink and patches, Legion. You should know that by now. And if you didn't, well, now you do. You took the fall. Did the time. Kept your mouth shut when the Feds offered deals."

He taps the envelope. "Three years, every member put in what they could. Some more than others." He doesn't need to say who contributed the most. I can guess. "House is yours. Paid for. No strings. We had the old trailer hauled away two days ago. Tried to clean up the shitty yard a bit when the new one dropped but..." He shrugs. Winces. "It's still a shitty yard."

I don't know what to say. Words stick in my throat. "I was... I was gonna burn it. That same night I got home."

Brick laughs, comes around the desk, and pulls me to my feet. His hand grips my shoulder, tight enough to anchor me to the moment. "Well, that would've sucked. An arson investigation would've really fucked up the timeline, so—" He claps me on the back hard enough to make me choke. "I'm glad ya didn't." Then he points at me. Flashes that smile that's been a winner with the women for five decades. "You're family now, Demon. And family means something. You take care of us, we take care of you."

He pulls me into an embrace, careful of the brand on my chest. It's brief but fierce. When he steps back, his eyes are suspiciously bright.

"Thank you," I manage, the words inadequate.

He nods, already turning away, uncomfortable with the moment. "Get the kid settled in. Take a day or two. Then... come find me. We'll talk business."

I gather the papers, the cash, my new life wrapped in manila. As I reach the door, Brick speaks again. "Legion."

I turn.

"Good to have you home."

I nod, not trusting my voice, and step out into the hallway.

Standing there, papers in hand, I feel something I haven't felt... well... *ever*.

Hope.

It's dangerous, that feeling. Hope is a luxury I can't afford. Not yet. Not with Destiny still missing, pregnant and alone. Not with Mercy still jumping at shadows. Not with Savannah wearing another man's ring.

But it's there all the same. Small. Fragile. Real.

One step at a time. One bullet at a time. One breath at a time. That's how I survive.

I tuck the envelope under my arm and go to find my sister.

Time to go home.

Mercy is still at the shootin' range. Her finger slides to the trigger. She breathes in. Holds. Exhales slow. The shot cracks across the yard. Fifty yards out, once again, a sign jerks and pings

"Fuck me," Diesel says, his voice low with admiration. "Think she's ready for her own Glock?" Diesel asks, pride warming his rough voice. He glances at me, grinning. "Been teaching her all week. Girl's got an eye."

I watch him watching her, this six-foot-five sergeant at arms with his scarred knuckles and dead-eye stare, looking at my little sister like she's the second coming. It hits me that she could do worse than having a mean motherfucker like Diesel on her side.

"Not today," I say, as Mercy pings another sign with a clean shot.

Diesel shrugs. "Your call. But she's got talent." He claps a heavy hand on Mercy's shoulder as she lowers the rifle. "Good shooting, Sis. You come back anytime you want."

"Come back?" Mercy's voice is flat, but I catch the confusion in it. The confusion hardening to anger as she turns to me.

Diesel realizes his mistake immediately. "Uh… I'm gonna go check on that thing. Inside. You know. The thing." He backs away, hands up, a big man suddenly unsure of his footing.

When he's gone, Mercy turns the full force of her stare on me. "What does he mean, *come back*?"

"Ya can't stay here, Mercy."

"Why not?"

"It's not a place for girls."

Wrong answer. Her face twists, flushing red with anger. "That's stupid! I've been here all week and nobody cared! Nobody ever cares where I am!" She gestures wildly with the rifle, not pointing it at me, but not exactly being careful either. "You ruin everything! *Everything*! I don't trust you. I don't trust anyone. And I never will again."

I catch her arm, not rough, but firm enough to stop the wild movement of the weapon. "Mercy. Please."

She tries to wrench free, but I hold on. Not to hurt. Just to keep her here. With me. For one more minute.

"Give me one more chance," I say. "And if I fuck it up today, you have every right to hate me. Blame me. Never speak to me again."

She goes still, looking at my hand on her arm. "That's stupid," she says finally, voice smaller. "Because you're all I've got left."

The words hit because they're true. "That's right. We're all we have now. Just each other. The last two Kanes standing."

She doesn't pull away, but she doesn't soften either. Just waits, watching me with those eyes too old for her face.

"Trust is just the slow death of hope," I tell her, the words coming from somewhere I didn't know existed. "Every time someone walks away, they take a piece of you with them. I know what that feels like and I'm standing here telling you, that's not what this is. That's not who I am."

"Since when?" Her voice is sharp as glass.

"Fuck's sake, kid. Give me a break. I'm doin' my best." I hold up the envelope as proof. "And for your fuckin' information—"

"What's that?" she interrupts, eyes narrowing at the manila paper.

"I'm not asking you to trust me," I say, lowering my voice. "Just to let me try again."

She stares at me, eyes lookin' me up and down with more calculation than some prisoners I did time with. I take the rifle from her hands, slow and careful. "Go put your helmet on," I say, pointing to my bike. "I'm gonna put this away and be right back."

Mercy folds her arms across her chest, making that mean mouth that reminds me too much of our mother. She's pouting, but at least she's not shooting.

Then she turns and stomps off toward the bike, each footfall a percussion of doubt.

I let out a breath. My brand is pounding. My head is pounding. My heart too.

That was a pretty big promise, and if I leave her again, she'll never forgive me.

I make a note of it.

. . .

The Montana wind kicks up dust devils that dance across the road as we ride. Mercy's small arms are locked around my waist, her helmet pressed against my back. Every time we hit a bump, she tightens her grip like she's afraid I'll disappear if she lets go.

I take the long way back to Drybone, not ready to show her what's waiting. The envelope burns in my jacket pocket—keys to something I'm not sure I deserve.

When we finally turn down our road, the gravel crunches under my tires. Sitting on the same twenty acres of scrubland is the new double-wide.

It's newer than anything my family has ever owned. And… it's nice. Looks a lot like the clubhouse, actually with both the roof and siding made of black-matte metal with a timber wainscot skirt of corrugated metal the color of rust. The shutters, door, and wide front porch are all made of timber stained the same color as the wainscoting.

It's kinda badass, outlaw, and trendy all in one go.

I kill the engine and we sit there on the bike, not moving.

"Where are we?" Mercy asks, voice muffled through her helmet.

"Home," I say, and the word feels strange in my mouth. Foreign.

I swing my leg over the bike and help her down. She pulls off the helmet, hair wild with static, and stares at the new trailer like it might be a mirage.

"What is this place?"

"Ours," I say, pulling the keys from the envelope. "The club got it for us."

Mercy doesn't move toward it. She just stands there, helmet dangling from her fingers, taking in the brand-new doublewide.

"It's nice," I offer. "Don't you think?"

She doesn't answer. Just walks forward slowly, like she's approaching a wild animal. Her eyes scan everything—

"Do you like it?" I ask.

No answer. Just that stare that's too old for her face.

I climb the steps, wood groaning under my weight, and unlock the door. It swings open without the screech I'm used to. No rust. No rot. Just clean hinges and the smell of new carpet.

Mercy follows me inside, and the difference between this and our old place hits hard. The living room is open and bright with that expensive wide-plank vinyl flooring that's so popular these days. There's even actual furniture—a couch that doesn't sag, a coffee table without cigarette burns, a TV mounted to the wall.

The kitchen has black appliances that weren't made before I was born. White cabinets. A refrigerator that doesn't sound like it's dyin'. Countertops void of knife marks or cigarette burns.

Mercy moves through the space like a ghost. She opens every cupboard, every drawer. Runs her fingers along the edges of counters. Turns on the faucet and watches water flow clear, not rust-colored.

I follow her down the hallway where she pushes open doors. Three bedrooms. One for each of us, with the third waiting for Destiny if she ever comes back. A bathroom with a shower that doesn't leak. Closets with actual doors.

She doesn't say a word through any of it. Just looks. Touches. Tests.

When she's seen everything, she walks back to the kitchen and stands in the center of it. Her small shoulders start to shake, and before I can reach her, she's crying—silent tears streaming down her face.

"Mercy?" I crouch down in front of her. "What's wrong? Don't you like it?"

She shakes her head, but I can't tell if that means no, she doesn't like it, or no, that's not why she's crying.

"Talk to me," I say, gentler than I knew I could be. "What's going on in that head of yours?"

She wipes her nose with the back of her hand. "Good things don't happen to me," she whispers. "Not things like this."

My chest tightens. "What do you mean?"

"The clubhouse was good," she says, "but that's different. That's inside my world. This—" she gestures around at the clean, new space "—this isn't. I don't belong here."

Something breaks inside me. How sad of a kid do you have to be—how utterly lost and hopeless—to see a shiny, brand-new home as something you don't deserve?

"Listen to me," I say, taking her small hands in mine. They're calloused in places no child's hands should be. "This is our new life. The club is our family now. Things are gonna be different."

She looks at me with those eyes that have seen too much. "You always say that."

"I know." The truth cuts. "But this time I have proof." I gesture around us. "This is real, Mercy. This is ours. And nobody's taking it away."

"Until they do," she whispers.

I shake my head. "Not this time."

"How do you know?"

"Because I paid for it already." The words come out harder than I meant. "Three years in a cage. That was the price. And I'd do it again if it means you get to have this."

Her eyes widen slightly. "You didn't do anything wrong. Destiny told me."

"It doesn't matter." I stand up, suddenly needing to move. "What matters is what happens next. We're gonna have a nice, easy summer, Merce. That's what happens next. You're gonna live here, in our new house, and have all the fun you want. And then, when summer's over, you're gonna go back to school and do your best."

"Why should I do my best in school? School is stupid."

"Because you're not gonna end up like Mama," I say, pacing the room. "You're not gonna end up like me. And you're damn sure not gonna end up like Destiny. And that's what school give you. It's an opportunity, Mercy. That's what school is. It's a way to change things. You're gonan have a nice, easy summer and then you're gonna go back to school in the fall and change things by doin' your best. We've got this new house now, I did my time, I'm patched in. Life is different. Things are different. And we're never goin' back to the way they were. That's my promise. I swear it on my fuckin' life. But change doesn't come easy. We gotta work for it, Mercy. We gotta *make* it happen."

She watches me pace, her tears drying on her cheeks.

"Poverty isn't just being broke," I tell her, the words coming from somewhere deep and dark. "It's the long, slow death of families. It's watching your mama work three jobs and still come home crying because the lights got shut off. It's learning to be hungry and callin' it normal."

I stop at the window, looking out at the scrubland that stretches to the horizon. "We grew up thinking we deserved nothing, so nothing is what we got. But that ends with us, Mercy. It ends today."

"How?" Her voice is so small.

"By *believing* we deserve better." I turn back to her. "By taking what's ours instead of waiting for someone to decide we're worth givin' it to."

She looks around the kitchen again, touching the edge of the counter like it might disappear. "What if I break it?"

"Then we'll fix it."

"What if I can't?"

"Then I will."

She takes a deep breath. "What if you leave again?"

The question hangs between us, heavy with all the promises I've already broken. I could lie. Tell her I never will. But we both know better.

"If I leave," I say slowly, "it won't be because I want to. And it won't be forever."

She nods, like this is an answer she can live with. Not perfect, but honest.

"The world's been trying to bury the Kanes for generations," I tell her. "Our grandpa died in a mine. Our mama died bringing you into the world. Destiny's out there somewhere, probably scared and alone. But we're still here. Still standing. And that means somethin'."

I reach out and brush a strand of hair from her face. "Home isn't just a place, Merce. It's having someone who looks for you when you're lost. Someone who fights for you when you can't fight for yourself."

"Is that what you do?" she asks.

"It's what I'm tryin' to do," I admit. "I'm not perfect at it. But I'm not stoppin' either."

She looks at me for a long moment, then walks to the refrigerator and opens it. Empty shelves gleam back at us.

"We need food," she says simply.

And just like that, we're moving forward.

One small step at a time.

"Yeah," I say, relief washing through me. "We do."

CHAPTER 10
SAVANNAH

I wake to the soft glow of dawn seeping through the wooden shutters. The light stretches across the ceiling in pale gold bands. Below, voices rise through the floorboards—sharp, insistent, unwelcome.

Marcus.

I roll onto my side, pressing my face into the cool pillow. The sage-colored sheets twist around my legs, evidence of another restless night. I haven't slept much after Legion.

The argument downstairs grows louder. Colt's voice cuts through, defensive and firm. They're discussing me, of course. Marcus wants to come up here, Cash is tellin' him no. Marcus has a hard time with rules. But here in the Ashby house, we have a pretty hard and fast one.

No one but family comes upstairs. Ever.

This bedroom might've been a stage all growing up, but these days it is mine, and mine alone. No photographs allowed. No social media tours. No carefully staged moments for followers to dissect. After twenty-three years of performin'—and the death of my mother—I carved out this one private corner.

I swing my legs over the edge of the bed, my bare feet meeting the wide-plank floor as the memory of Legion's hands on my skin lingers from the dream Marcus just pulled me out of, and I head to the closet.

The door opens silently. I walk in, scanning the rows of hanging clothes—endless skirts and prairie dresses, boots lined up like soldiers. The uniform of the Ashby heiress, curated for maximum engagement. Hashtag AuthenticRanchLife.

But I'm not in here lookin' for clothes. I'm lookin' for secrets.

At the back of the closet, behind winter coats and formal gowns, sits a small panel. I slide the pocket door open, revealing the elevator door. It opens when I use my mother's code and inside there is a single button to press. The doors close and the elevator descends smoothly. Forty feet down, past foundation and earth, into solid rock.

It's been a while since the overwhelmin' urge to see the treasures down here were strong enough to make me actually descend, but today, I crave these secrets like they are life itself.

The safe room is exactly as I saw it last. Temperature-controlled. Enough airflow to create a wind. Windowless, with dim lightin' that won't damage the hundreds of thousands of photographs that live here in negative form. All cataloged, preserved, and protected.

There are thousands more on contact sheets and archival paper.

I walk between the shelves, past boxes labeled with dates and subjects. Twenty-three years of my childhood, all neatly archived. Every milestone, every "candid" moment, every outfit change.

Sometimes I do look at them—not recently. But sometimes.

Today, though, all I want is what's in the safe.

It stands against the far wall, ancient and imposing. Eight feet tall, six feet wide, the combination dial is worn smooth from decades of use. It's been here since before the house was built on top of it. A relic from the early 1900s, something that belongs in a black-and-white bank-heist film.

I stand before it, turning the dial with practiced precision. The mechanisms inside click and shift. It's filled with private treasures. But I'm not here for those, either.

I'm here for The Book.

I lift it carefully, lovin' the weight of it in my hands. The red leather cover is soft from handling, the pages thick and heavy.

Then I take it over to the velvet couch in the corner, lower myself down, and open it up.

The first page stares back at me like it always does—a single black and white image of a dust-streaked toddler squattin' in the dirt. Blond hair catches the sunlight, standing up in wild tufts. His small hands grip a matchbox car, but his eyes—those impossibly blue eyes when not dulled to monochrome—look directly at the camera.

Legion Kane. Maybe three years old.

I turn the page with care. The progression is familiar—close-ups of those eyes, narrowed against prairie sun. A series of candids where he doesn't know he was being watched.

Climbing fences, throwing rocks at nothing, sleeping under a tree with his arm flung over his face.

The pages whisper as I turn them. Eleanor arranged these photos by some internal logic only she understood. Mostly age, but there's several series that span decades, and then the progression will loop back on itself and seemingly start over.

Here's Legion at seven, his school photo taken from an angle no school photographer would choose—slightly below, catching the light in his lashes, making him look celestial and feral all at once.

Then Legion at nine, ten, eleven—leaning against fences, looking outward, always outward, as if searching for hole in a fence he can't ever escape. His features sharpening with each passing year, baby softness giving way to angles that now cut like glass.

Me and Legion, fourteen and sixteen. She knew. She'd found us... somehow. Her camera capturing moments we thought were ours alone. Kisses stolen behind hay bales. Our bodies stretched beneath stars. My head on his chest, his hand in my hair.

She never said a word. Never confronted me. Just... *documented*.

My fingers tremble slightly as I turn to the next section. After I left for college when I was eighteen and he was twenty. After I stopped meetin' him at the silo.

Four years of silence between us while I played the

part of perfect college equestrian at Emory & Henry—good lighting, good posture, just enough ribbons to keep my mother's social timeline humming along.

Four years.

Four missing years where I had no contact with him at all. It nearly killed me, but were in our we-can't-do-this-anymore era and I was determined to...

To what, Savannah? Prove that you could live without him?

What a waste of time.

Anyway, it was during these missing years that the photos changed from candid shots to composed, intentional, and intimate portraits.

Intimate. I hate that word.

Legion is now in Mother's Drybone studio. Professional lighting catching the planes of his face and the stretch of his shoulders. The ink that started appearing when he was sixteen grows as I turn pages. The battle on his chest, the conquering of demons on his back go from being an image to being a composition.

Each photo reveals more than the last.

Shirt discarded in this one. Jeans riding low in the next. In some, there's nothing but shadow preserving his dignity.

She never photographed his dick, but she got his ass. Many times. All the photos are black and white. Artistic and beautiful.

And in every single one, his eyes hold the same hollow sadness.

Did she pay him? Is that why he did this? Was it money?

I've studied these pages for years and still don't know.

When I reach the last photo, I hold my breath. I always do.

None of the photos are dated, but this one *is*. It's not her handwriting, either. It's his.

Six months before Eleanor died, she and Legion were in an Ashby truck together. They were on a road, it's summer. Not sure which highway, though I've searched them all over the past seven years, trying to figure it out.

The windows are down. Hair blowin' all over the place. They're taking a couple's selfie as Legion drives across the sun-drenched badlands.

They are both smilin'. Mother looks... happy. Forty-eight years old and radiant beside him.

I pause.

I reflect.

I accept.

And then I close the book, resting my palm on its cover.

This book isn't motherly.

It isn't innocent.

It isn't okay.

It was never shared. Never monetized. Never digitized.

The one secret Eleanor Ashby never spun into gold was Legion Kane.

The one child she photographed relentlessly and *didn't* use to make money.

Him.

Not me.

Him.

To the world, she was the mother who made me a brand.

In private, she was the woman who collected a boy like butterfly wings pinned to velvet.

I have questions I will never get answered.

Because only two people know what this book truly is and one of them is dead. I will never ask Legion about this book. Ever. Some secrets should stay buried, even as they haunt us.

I get up, slip the Book of Legion back into the safe, and lock away the secrets that feel too heavy to carry upstairs.

My fingers linger on the dial before I turn away and then the elevator hums as it returns me to my closet, to my life, to the performance.

By afternoon, I'm in the outdoor arena, my heels and lower legs pressing the hidden buttons on Cassia's warm body that will tell her to yield, or shoulder in, or half-pass as we practice the only thing I got out of college—dressage skills.

Meaningless in the grand scheme of things, but very impressive when dropped into an Instagram reel with trending music.

That's not why I do it, though I do share videos like that on occasion.

I do it because dressage is a partnership between horse and rider at the highest level of trust. No words are spoken. You're not allowed to speak during a dressage test. No clicking, no whoas, no words of encouragement when your equine partner does it just right. The dressage horse is the only animal in the world that has learned to be fluent in a language where hands are syllables, and legs are words, and heels are sentences.

My mare's hooves stir dust that floats golden in the sunlight. My instructor, Madeline, nods approvingly from the center of the ring. "Beautiful extension, Savannah. Now collect her and prepare for the flying change."

I gather the reins, feeling Cassia's powerful muscles respond beneath me. This is the only honest conversation I have most days—between my body and hers, a language of pressure and release. No words needed. No lies possible.

The rhythm of her hooves against packed earth drowns out everything else until I spot him—Marcus—leaning against the black fence rail, arms crossed, watching. His pressed shirt looks ridiculous against the backdrop of working ranch buildings. His polished shoes already dusty.

"Let's take a break," Madeline suggests, noting my sudden tension.

I ignore her, asking Cassia for a flying change instead. Left to right, her legs switching mid-air with balletic precision. I want Marcus to see me controlling something this powerful, this beautiful. I want him to understand I'm not just a pretty face for his campaign posters.

"Savannah." His voice carries across the arena. "We need to talk."

Madeline looks between us, professional enough not to show curiosity. "Perhaps we should end early today?"

"That would be best," I say, patting Cassia's neck. "Thank you, Madeline."

I dismount in one fluid motion, my boots hitting the ground with a soft thud. Taking Cassia's reins, I lead her toward the barn without acknowledging Marcus. His footsteps follow behind me, crushing gravel.

"You've been avoiding me all day," he says, catching up.

"I've been busy."

"Too busy for your fiancé? After what happened last weekend?"

I keep walking, focusing on Cassia's dark mane turning copper in the sunlight. The barn door looms ahead, promising temporary sanctuary.

"Savannah." His hand catches my elbow. "My father is furious. Three donors pulled their support this morning."

I stop so abruptly that Cassia tosses her head in surprise. Turning to face Marcus, I drop my voice low enough that the stable hands can't hear.

"If you do not leave right now and stay away until I call you back, I will break things off publicly."

His eyes widen, then narrow. The political calculation happens instantly behind them—what it would cost him if I walked away. Millions of followers. The Ashby name. The land. The money.

"Is that a threat?" he asks, voice smooth as river stones.

I say nothing. Just stare at him with the emptiness I

learned from my mother's camera lens. Sometimes silence is the only power we have.

He straightens his cuffs—a nervous habit I've cataloged along with all his other tells. "We'll talk when you're being reasonable."

I watch him walk away, his shoulders stiff under expensive fabric. Only when his car disappears down the drive do I exhale, pressing my forehead against Cassia's warm neck. She smells like sweat, and summer dust, and everything real.

Inside the barn's cool shadow, I untack her methodically. Each motion practiced until it feels like prayer. The leather saddle creaks as I lift it to the rack, and something in me creaks too—some weight I've been carrying too long.

I bathe Cassia until her coat gleams, speaking softly to her about nothing. The hose water runs cool over her legs, washing away arena dust. She stands patient, trusting, as I focus on her and only her. This fourteen-hundred-pound animal who could crush me, but chooses to be my ballet partner instead.

After grooming, I turn her out to graze in the east pasture. Watching her for longer than necessary. She lowers her head to the grass, peaceful and unburdened by expectations.

I don't make a conscious decision. My feet just carry me to the Range Rover, no need for keys, I leave them in glove box when I'm at home. I don't change out of my riding clothes—the white breeches, the tall boots still flecked with water from Cassia's bath. My hair is coming loose from its braid and I make no move to fix it.

The engine purrs to life, expensive and obedient. I back out too fast, gravel spittin' under my tires. Cash's truck is by the main house. He'll know I've gone somewhere.

Let him wonder.

I drive without admitting where I'm going, even to myself. But my hands know. They turn the wheel toward the county road, away from town. Toward the creek bed that separates Ashby land from Kane land.

The road narrows, trees pressing closer on either side. My hands grip the wheel tighter. The diamond on my left hand catches the sunlight, throwing prisms across the dashboard. I should have taken it off. I should turn around. I should call Marcus and apologize.

I don't.

The trailer comes into view and I hit the brakes so hard the seatbelt locks across my chest.

What the hell?

Where Legion's dilapidated single-wide *should be* stands something else entirely—a brand-new double-wide with fresh charcoal black siding, a wide covered porch, and… shutters.

What the actual fuck is happening here?

I look around. Did I take a wrong turn?

No. There's the Kane mailbox. Still sad and still crooked.

Where the hell did this house come from?

I sit frozen, engine idling. Part of me wants to reverse, pretend I never came. But then the door opens, and out bounces Mercy.

She waves at me from the porch. Smiling.

I don't think I've ever seen that child smile.

"Hey, Savannah!" she calls. "Come inside and see our new house!"

CHAPTER 11

SAVANNAH

I kill the engine but remain frozen, studying this alien patch of suburban perfection that's somehow replaced Legion's familiar broken-down trailer.

Mercy skips down the porch steps, all wild energy and pure delight in ragged cutoff shorts and what must be Legion's ancient t-shirt, the fabric drowning her tiny frame, carrying his presence like a lingering shadow. "Come on! We got actual furniture and everything!" Her voice quivers with the kind of raw excitement that makes my chest tight.

The three-carat diamond weighing down my left hand might as well be shackles when I step out. The soles of my riding boots crunch against fresh gravel as I gently close the Range Rover's door.

"I like your pants. You look like you like you do on socials," Mercy says, studying my four-hundred-dollar breeches and five-thousand-dollar custom boots.

I blow out a breath, instant regret about coming

143

here. And I would leave… but I can't. Not with this new trailer staring back at me.

"It's nice, right?" Mercy asks.

I nod. "It is. Where did it come from?"

"Come on! Come inside," she says, not answering my question as she takes my hand and starts pulling me towards the porch.

I follow her up the fresh-built steps, cross the small, but ample porch, and get blasted with air conditioning the moment I cross the threshold.

Inside, it's open concept—kitchen melting into living room, everything immaculate and untouched. There are no staged corners or meticulously arranged scenes like my Instagram feed demands. Just clean, functional space with furniture meant for real life, not harvesting engagement metrics.

"Look at this!" Mercy yanks me toward the kitchen, practically levitating with joy. "Dishwasher AND automatic ice! No more gas station runs!"

I almost mention the designer countertops—that ingrained social media reflex—but she's already pulling me down the hallway, her small fingers warm and eager between mine.

"My room!" She flings a door wide with theatrical flair. "I see your house on Instagram all the time. Yours is gigantic, but look—sage walls! Just like that one guest cabin you guys have on your property!"

Something breaks quietly in my chest. This precious, untamed little girl follows my carefully constructed lies. Not only that, she has opinions about them.

The charity events, the couture outfits, the picture-perfect moments with my politically groomed fiancé—all of it as artificial as my follower demographics.

"Legion got me this too!" She gestures proudly at a cork board plastered with equestrian magazine clippings—some torn from publications featuring my sponsored content. "Says maybe I can take riding lessons. Like in your stories! I've always wanted a horse. You have one, Cassia, right? I want one like yours."

I blow out a breath. My horse cost half a million dollars as a barely-broke three-year-old. I got her when I was seventeen, one year before I took her to college with me. She came from Germany. Like… has-an-EU-passport came from Germany.

The guilt I feel about all that hits instantly.

I have too much.

She has so little.

Mercy continues her enthusiastic tour, treating each modern fixture and organized closet like buried treasure.

I've never known Legion in normal spaces. Only secret places—the grain silo, the hidden creek, anywhere we could pretend reality didn't exist. But this is real. His world. His sanctuary. His baby sister who follows my filtered fantasy life and dreams of horses she's never been allowed to touch.

"Want to see Legion's new room?" Mercy asks, bouncing with anticipation. "He got a new bed too."

I peek into Legion's room, unable to stop myself. But quickly turn away and go back down the hallway to the living room. He and I aren't dating. Hell, I'm engaged—the whole idea of dating Legion is ridiculous.

We're hookups.

Hookups that have never happened in this trailer, or the last, actually. And I don't know what he does while he and I aren't together—have never known, aside from posing suggestively for my mother, that is. And there could be evidence in that room of some other woman who meets his needs while I sit up in my castle lookin' out on my kingdom.

As I'm thinking all this, I'm also studying the pristine living room sofa—tan fabric with throw pillows that match the curtains. It looks like it came from a catalog, like someone tried to stage the perfect middle-class home.

"Legion's not here," Mercy announces, flopping onto the couch with the kind of comfortable abandon I haven't felt in my own body since I was her age. "He's at work."

"Work?" The word feels foreign in my mouth when attached to Legion. "What the hell does he do for 'work'?" I don't know why it comes out like that— prickly. But it does. Have I ever known Legion to have a 'job'?

Well, I'm pretty sure he did have jobs as a teenager. He always had money. Not a lot, but he bought that dirt bike with his own money, I do remember him saying that. So he did work. I just… never asked *where*, I guess. Then, as adults, I just assumed it was something… illegal. Something to do with the club.

"I dunno where he works," Mercy shrugs. "The Club, I think. He leaves early. Comes back late. It pays the bills."

Pays the bills. It's a phrase straight out of his mouth, not Mercy's. She's just repeating him.

I perch on the edge of an armchair, keeping my posture straight like Mama taught me. My diamond catches the light, throwing prisms across the wall. I notice Mercy staring at it, then quickly looking away.

I've been here plenty of times over the past three years. To help Destiny. Then Mercy, once Destiny left. To drop off food, or pick up laundry and bring it back, once cleaned.

But all those times—every single one of those times—Legion was in prison.

I have never been *inside his space.*

And now here I am. And I don't know how to process it, so the manners kick in. "The place is really nice, Mercy," I say, when I realize she's looking at me, waiting for… *words.*

"I know!" She bounces up, energy crackling through her small frame. "When school starts again in the fall, I'm gonna go to school every day. No more skippin'. I will have new clothes and the new supplies. Kids won't make fun of me no more. And I'll bring my own lunch too!" She pauses her excitement here to give me a serious look. "We have real food in the fridge, not just beans and soda."

"Beans and soda," I say softly. Yep. That was all that was in there the first time I brought food.

"Wanna see something cool?" Without waiting for an answer, Mercy darts down the hallway and returns with a brand new backpack—purple with silver stars. "All my school stuff is new. And look—" She pulls out a lunch box with horses on it. "Legion says I need to eat actual food, not just whatever kids give me."

"It's super cute," I tell her. "I love it."

"Oh! And I have all kinds of new friends at the Club."

"New... *friends*?"

"Oh, you haven't met them yet!" Mercy's eyes light up. "They're super nice. Brick looks really scary—he's got this face like thunder—but he gave me this cool knife block for the kitchen." She points to a wooden block on the counter filled with gleaming kitchen knives. "And he always brings me candy, but he checks with Legion first 'cause sometimes I lie and say I already brushed my teeth."

She says this so casually, like it's perfectly normal to have a biker gang as your BFF. I force a smile. "That's... thoughtful."

"His bike is the coolest thing ever. It's got these skulls on the handlebars that light up red at night. He let me sit on it once when Legion wasn't lookin'."

"Ummm... OK."

"Roach is super twitchy, like this—" Mercy demonstrates by wiggling her fingers rapidly and blinking fast. "But he's super smart too. He taught me chess! Says I have a 'tactical mind,' whatever that means."

She hops up and moves to the window, demonstrating. "He showed me how to check if someone messed with our locks or windows. See these little bits of tape? If they're broken, someone came in while we were gone."

I feel sick. "That's... an interesting skill."

"He has like ten different phones, but never takes pictures. I asked why once and he said 'plausible deniability' which sounds made up." She laughs these words out, moving to the kitchen to get a juice box from the fridge.

"Ledger wears glasses like my teacher, but way scarier. He brought me these math workbooks 'cause I'm behind in school." She takes a long sip. "He taught me to count money the right way. Says I need to know if someone's shortin' me. I don't know what that means, but I can count really fast now. Twenty, forty, sixty, eighty, one hundred. Twenty, forty, sixty, eighty, two hundred. That's how you do it."

I try to keep my expression neutral. "Math is important."

"Diesel is my favorite though. He's HUGE!" She spreads her arms wide. "Like a bear! But he's super nice. Taught me how to shoot better—says my aim was good but my stance was garbage."

"He taught you to… *shoot*?" My voice rises despite my effort to keep calm.

"Yeah! At the range behind the clubhouse. I'm really good now." She says this with such innocent pride. "He checks on me when Legion works late. Brings me ice cream sometimes."

Again with this 'job' thing. I can't help asking. "What does Legion do again? For work?"

Mercy scrunches her face. "I told you, I dunno. Club stuff? He comes home smelling like gasoline sometimes. Or smoke." She shrugs. "Chains drew me these cool pictures—wanna see?"

Before I can answer, she's pulling a folder from her

backpack, showing me intricate drawings of flowers and animals—clearly done by someone with serious artistic talent. But they all look like tattoo sheets.

"And Butch is teaching me to make a fist the right way. See?" She demonstrates, tucking her thumb outside her fingers. "Says girls need to know how to throw a punch that won't break their hand."

"Mercy—" I start, not sure what to say.

"Oh! And Ratchet showed me how to check tire pressure and oil. Says everyone should know basic maintenance." She mimics turning a wrench. "His hands are always dirty but he's good with engines."

I sit there, stunned by how thoroughly the Badlands MC has integrated themselves into this child's life. I was here, dropping off food and clean clothes just a couple of weeks ago. She didn't know any of them. They never came with food. They never came with clean clothes.

They were not here. *I was.*

These men are criminals, drug runners, violent enforcers. They're teaching money math and bike maintenance to a nine-year-old girl. How to shoot and make a fist.

This is not a life for a child.

"They sound... interesting," I manage.

"They're the best!" Mercy flops back onto the couch. "Way better than those kids at school. They say mean things about Legion sometimes. Call him Demon Kane." Her voice drops. "I punched Jimmy Larson for that. I got suspended, but Brick said I did good."

The realization hits me like cold water: *This* is Legion's world.

Not the silo where we meet in secret.

Not the photos in the book.

This is the part of him I never saw.

The part of him he never let me see.

This trailer, this child, these dangerous men who bring math books and teach a little girl to shoot—this is his reality.

And I have absolutely no place in it.

And now that I think about it, neither does Mercy.

CHAPTER 12
LEGION

The bike thrums between my legs, engine hot from the long haul back from Terry. Six hours of warehouse inventory with Ledger, counting shit that isn't on any manifest. My shoulders ache. My brand still burns under my shirt, the healing has been worse than the actual moment of branding.

Plastic bags of Chinese food hang from my grip, swinging as I take the last turn onto our road. Got Mercy those sugar donuts she likes. The ones dusted with cinnamon that leave her fingerprints everywhere.

I almost stop the bike when I see the Range Rover, white and gleaming in my dirt driveway like some alien spacecraft landed while I was gone. Savannah's ride. I'd know it anywhere—seen it enough times on her Instagram, parked outside fancy hotels, designer shopping bags arranged just so on the hood.

I kill the engine, let silence fill the space where my heartbeat should be. The food bags crinkle as I tighten my grip.

What the fuck is she doin' here?

Five days since the silo.

Five days since I cut her loose, really expecting it to be the end this time.

Five days of nothing but the ache in my chest and the memory of her skin.

They know I'm here. You don't sneak up on anyone riding this bike. The door opens before I can reach for it.

"Legion!" Mercy's face appears, grinning wide. "We have a visitor!"

Like I could miss the six-figure SUV parked out front.

I step inside, keeping my face blank. Savannah sits on our couch, all honey-blonde and polished in her riding clothes. Tight white pants. Tall black boots. Hair pulled back in a low bun. The ring is back on her finger, diamond catching light like it's showing off.

"Brought dinner," I say, holding up the bags. My voice sounds normal. Doesn't give away the ache in my chest.

Mercy bounces over, snatching the bags from my hands. "Chinese? *Yes!*" She peers inside. "Did you get—"

"Sugar donuts are in the bottom bag."

She grins, already digging for them. "Savannah came to see the new place!"

"So I see." I look at Savannah, really look at her. Something's off. Her smile doesn't reach her eyes. There's tension in her shoulders I recognize—the kind she gets when she's trying not to crack.

"I was just in the neighborhood," she says. Bullshit. Nobody's "just in the neighborhood" of Kane land. We're the wrong side of everywhere.

"Nice of you to drop by." I keep my tone even. "Wasn't expecting company, or I'd have brought more food."

"Oh, I'm not staying for dinner." Her smile tightens a fraction. The diamond flashes again as she tucks hair behind her ear.

Mercy hauls the food to the kitchen, already opening containers, the smell of fried rice and kung pao chicken filling the air. "This is so much better than what we had at the clubhouse," she calls over her shoulder.

I watch Savannah flinch at the word "clubhouse." There's a story there. Something happened while I was gone.

"Mercy," I say, not taking my eyes off Savannah, "give us a minute, will ya?"

"But the food—"

"It'll still be there." I reach out my hand to Savannah. "Let's go for a walk."

She hesitates, then takes my hand. Her fingers are cool against mine. I can feel the ring pressing into my skin.

"Don't touch my food," I warn Mercy. "I'll be right back."

"Whatever." She's already got a pair of chopsticks in her hand, rooting through the containers. "I'm not making any promises."

I lead Savannah outside, onto the porch, into the purple dusk. The air smells like dust and sage. Her perfume cuts through it—something expensive, subtle.

The moment we're alone, I drop her hand.

"What are ya doin' here, Savannah?"

The diamond on her finger catches the last light of day.

Three carats of bullshit.

Three years of my life.

All of it feels weighed and measured in that stone.

"This place looks... different," she says, gesturing at the new trailer. Her fingers tremble slightly, like she wants to touch the outside to make sure it's real. "Last time I was here, it was—"

"A rusted-out piece of shit?" The words are bitter and come out mean. "Yeah, well. Now it's not. What do ya really want, Savannah?"

She takes a step back, boot heel clicking against the fresh wood of the porch. "I wanna know where it came from. How you afforded it. How it got here so fast." Her eyes narrow. "And who exactly are these men from the clubhouse teaching Mercy all these new skills she's been braggin' about?"

Oh. I think to myself. *I do not think so, Miss Ashby.* "Let me be real clear." My voice drops low. "Mercy is *my* sister. Not yours. You don't get have opinions about how I raise her just because you dropped off groceries while I was gone."

"I just don't think it's a good idea." Her voice shakes a little. Surprised at my challenge. "Having Mercy around criminal bikers like—"

"Like *what*?" I lean in close. Let her see exactly what three years inside did to my eyes. Let her see the darkness that grew there, fed by concrete walls and fluorescent lights that never died. "*I'm* a criminal biker, Savannah. Did you forget that part while you were picking out china patterns?"

I grab her left hand, shove it up between us. The diamond shines unnaturally bright, like this moment was staged by Eleanor Ashby herself. "You lost all right to ask those questions the moment you put this ring on. You wanna know about the clubhouse? About who's teaching Mercy what? About where the money came from?"

She tries to pull away, but I hold tighter. Feeling her pulse race against my fingertips.

"Those are *family* questions, Savannah."

My voice starts hard, but it goes soft at the end when I say her name. I don't wanna be mad at her. I don't wanna hate her. Savannah Ashby is the only woman I've ever wanted in all my life. She's the one.

But she made her choice and now she has to live with it.

So this is what I tell her.

"You chose the mansion lights over midnight rides, Savannah. Chose diamond rings over chain links. I spent three years in darkness dreaming about you underneath me as the starlight dusted your skin. And while I was doin' that, you were busy turning yourself into something I don't recognize."

She lets out a breath and her eyes go sad.

But I keep going. Because I got shit to say.

If she stays away, I'll get over it. I'll *make myself* get over it. I'll look back at that last night in the silo as the perfect ending.

Not a happy one, but I never expected one of those.

If she stays away.

If she comes around, well that's another matter. If

she keeps comin' around, she's gonna kill me slowly. One moment at a time.

I'll *never* get over it.

I'll never get over *her*.

This will turn me mean and evil.

And I'm halfway there already. Have been since the day I was born. I can't risk the 'casual' nature of our past relationship.

Not anymore. It's not workin' for me.

"That's the thing about choices, Savannah." I look her straight in the eyes for this last part. "They don't just change your future. They burn your past to ash. And darlin', we're nothing but embers right now. Not the kind that spark up with the right wind, but the kind that die out slowly over time."

"You want me to leave."

It's not a question, but I answer it anyway. "No, Savannah. That's not what I want. I wanna keep you forever. But I'm done sharing, ya understand? I'm done bein' your dirty little secret. I don't like it. I never did. But if you're movin' on, then I'm movin' on too."

I pick up her hand again. Show her the ring. Her ring. The one she took off the last time we met up and then put it right back on when she got home.

Like I don't mean anything to her.

I'm just a hookup.

She's listening to me, I can tell by the way her nose crinkles up. She's thinking.

Do I believe she loves this senator's son more than me?

Fuck no. I don't even think she likes him.

But she will run back to that family money—to the mansion, and the land, and the horses, and the cattle, and the security of it all.

Yeah, she will.

And I just can't stand for that.

Because I can't give her that. Ever. I'll never be able to give her that. So either she wants *me*, or she wants her lifestyle.

If she chose the life, I wouldn't even hate her for it. I mean, I hope she does. Because picturing Savanah Ashby living in my new trailer is pretty much the saddest thing I can think of right now.

She doesn't deserve this. She deserves better.

And to be quite frank about shit, she's way too good for me. She's knows it, I know it, Cash knows it. That's why he gave me that warning.

"You want me to walk away, don't you, Legion?"

I'm too busy dyin' over the way she says my name to respond, so she just keeps going.

"Don't even bother denying it. I can see it all over your face. You wouldn't even know what to do with me if I was truly yours. *Only* yours."

She's not wrong.

"But I'm gonna have my say," she continues. "If you get to throw your midnight rides in my face, then I get to throw my love in yours."

Love.

Such a small word for the thing that's been killing me since I was fourteen.

"I love you," she says again, stepping closer. "I've loved you since I was twelve years old singing in that silo. I loved you when I was fifteen and gave you the most precious thing I had to offer. I loved you through four years of college, and three years of silence. Through engagement photos and charity galas and every single fucking Instagram post."

I don't move. Can't.

"I'll give it up," she whispers, and now her voice changes, becomes something harder. Something I recognize. "All of it. The car, the horses, the ranch—everything. I'll sign it over to Cash and walk away."

The world stops spinning for a second. Savannah Ashby without her inheritance is like a bird without wings. It's her protection, her power, the only thing that's ever truly been hers.

"But I want you to walk away too," she adds, and her eyes hold mine. "From the clubhouse."

And there it is. The trade.

"You want me to leave the Badlands." It's not a question. My hand moves unconsciously to my chest, to the brand still raw beneath my shirt. The mark I earned with three years of my life.

"Yes." One syllable, no hesitation. "If I walk away from my family, you walk away from yours."

It's a fair deal. Too fair. Which means it's impossible.

"If I did that," I ask slowly, "you'd get on the back of my bike, let me take you somewhere where you know absolutely no one—where I know absolutely no one—and you would start over with me?"

She nods, and there's not a single shadow of doubt in her eyes.

I shake my head, almost laughing. "And how exactly

would I support us, princess? What would I do for work with a prison record and no club backing me?" I gesture at the trailer behind us. "This? This is club money. That job I have? Club connections. You think I can just walk into some town and get hired as what—a fucking accountant?"

The fairy tale she's spinning falls apart against the sharp edges of reality. She doesn't understand what it means to have nothin'. To *be* nothin'.

"You think we'll rent some cute little apartment? That I'll bring home flowers while you—what? Wait tables? Post pictures of your breakfast for sponsors?" I'm being cruel now, but she needs to hear it. "The moment you step off that property without your name on it, you're just another pretty girl with empty pockets."

"I have money of my own," she says, but her voice wavers.

"For how long? A year? Two? And then what?" I step closer. "And what about Mercy? I just leave her here while we run off to play house?"

Something in Savannah's face shifts, and I know I've hit a nerve. She hadn't thought about Mercy.

"She could come—"

"To live how? On what? In a world where she has no one but us?" I shake my head. "You don't understand what it means to have nothing to fall back on. No safety net. No rich brother to bail you out when things get hard. This shitty twenty acres of scrub is all I got, Savannah. This new trailer is a dream come true. I get it, I understand what you're saying. And... it's even fucking reasonable. But I'm not walking out on my land."

She shakes her head and huffs out a breath. "But you want me to do it."

"No," I say firmly, taking her face in my hands. "I want what is best for you. And this?" I pan to the land and the trailer. "This isn't it."

"But it's good enough for you. It's good enough for Mercy."

"Savannah—"

But before I can say anything else, she presses her fingertips against my mouth.

"I'm going home to change," she says softly. "I feel ridiculous standing here like this." Her fingers trail down from my lips to my chest, resting right over the brand I took for my brothers.

She doesn't know it's there. Doesn't know I've already carved another name on my heart. And her touch, light as it is, hurts.

"But you'll know where to find me at midnight."

She steps back, and for a second, I see something in her eyes I've never seen before. Not the careful calculation of an Ashby or the practiced seduction of our silo nights. Something wilder. Something that scares me more than prison ever did.

Then she's leaving. Walking back to her Range Rover. The engine purrs to life, expensive and certain, just like everything else in her world.

I stand on my porch, feeling the night settle around me, wondering what kind of man I am—the kind who follows a woman into a dream that can't possibly last, or the kind who stays with the only family that ever truly wanted him.

I go inside and start counting the minutes to midnight.

At a quarter to twelve, I check on Mercy. She's sprawled across her bed, one arm dangling toward the floor, the other still clutching that damn BB gun like it's a teddy bear. I adjust her blanket, careful not to wake her. On her nightstand sits the fortune cookie from dinner, still unopened.

"Be back soon," I whisper.

Outside, the night air hits good. Stars punch through the black, cold and sharp. I take the old footpath down past the dried-up creek bed, my boots crunching on stones that have felt my weight a thousand times before.

The silo rises against the horizon like a sentinel. Ten minutes by foot from my door, but it might as well be another world.

The place where damnation and light begin.

My pulse is jumpin'. I'm five minutes early when I reach the clearing. The metal shell gleams silver in the moonlight, worn but standing. Like me.

Then I hear it—hoofbeats. Coming fast.

Savannah appears at the edge of the trees, Cassia's dark form moving like liquid shadow across the field. She doesn't slow until the last moment, then slides off before the horse fully stops, her feet hitting the ground running.

She's wearing a short dress, buttoned down the front, white cotton that catches the moonlight. Just like when we were kids. Just like the first time.

"You came," she breathes, stopping three feet away, chest rising and falling.

"Always do," I say, my voice rough.

The space between us burns away in seconds. We collide like we're trying to break each other, mouths hungry, hands desperate. I back her against the curved metal wall of the silo, the steel cool against my palms as I cage her between my arms.

I press my mouth against her neck, biting down on the soft skin where her pulse jumps.

Her fingers claw at my belt. "Legion…"

I press my hips against hers, letting her feel how hard I am. "Feel that? That's what you do to me. I wanna be inside you."

She moans, her head falling back against the metal. "Legion…"

"You want my fingers first?" I ask, already hiking up her dress, finding bare skin. No underwear. Fuck. "Or you want me to bend you over right here, where anyone could see?"

"Fingers," she gasps. "Then everything. All of you."

I slip my hand between her legs, finding her already slick and ready. "So fucking wet for me," I murmur, sliding two fingers inside her. She arches, a sound catching in her throat. "You think about this while you're wearing his ring? Think about me fucking you while he talks politics?"

"Yes," she admits, shameless, her eyes locked on mine. "Every day."

I curl my fingers inside her, finding that spot that makes her eyes roll back. "Tell me what you want."

"I want you to fuck me until I can't remember my

own name," she says, voice ragged. "Until all I know is yours."

My cock strains against my jeans, aching to be freed. I withdraw my fingers, bring them to my mouth, and taste her. "Sweet as I remember."

She reaches down, unbuttoning my jeans, wrapping her fingers around me. "Big as I remember," she says with a wicked smile.

I groan as she strokes me, slow and deliberate. "Keep that up and this'll be over before it starts."

"Then don't wait," she whispers, hiking one leg around my hip.

I lift her, pressing her back against the silo. She wraps both legs around my waist as I position myself at her entrance. The head of my cock slides against her wetness, and we both gasp.

"Say my name," I demand, hovering at the edge of pushing in.

"Legion," she breathes.

"Again."

"Legion," louder this time.

I thrust into her in one smooth motion, burying myself deep. "Fuck," I groan, the tight heat of her nearly undoin' me. "So perfect. So fucking perfect around my cock."

She cries out, her nails digging into my shoulders through my shirt. "Don't stop. Please don't stop."

I begin to move, driving into her against the hard metal shell. Each thrust pushes a little sound from her throat, half-moan, half-sob.

"This what you needed?" I growl against her ear.

"This what you've been missing? My cock filling you up while your fancy fiancé sleeps alone?"

"Yes," she gasps, meeting each thrust. "Only you. It's only ever been you."

I shift my angle, hitting deeper, and she throws her head back, nearly screaming. "That's it, princess. Let me hear you. Let everyone fucking hear you."

Her inner walls clench around me as she starts to come undone. "Legion, I'm—I'm gonna—"

"Come for me," I command, my rhythm relentless. "Come on my cock like the good girl you are."

She's moanin' my name, over and over, her body tightening around me, trembling on the edge—then —light.

Everywhere.

Flashlight beams cut through the darkness, blinding us. The unmistakable sound of shotguns cocking echoes across the field.

"Get the fuck off my sister." Cash's voice, cold as steel.

Savannah screams as I'm ripped away from her, my body suddenly empty of her warmth. Rough hands grab my shoulders, yanking me backward. I stumble, still half-exposed, disoriented by the sudden light and separation.

"No!" Savannah shrieks, pulling her dress down. "Stop it! Cash, stop it!"

I can make out shapes now—Cash, Wyatt, and Marcus, their faces twisted with rage. Behind them, ranch hands with rifles and flashlights form a half-circle. A fucking firing squad.

"Savannah, come here. Now." Cash's voice leaves no room for argument.

"I'm not going anywhere with you!" She tries to move toward me, but Wyatt blocks her path.

"You fucking animal," Marcus spits, advancing on me. "Couldn't stay away, could you?"

I try to speak, but something—someone—hits me from behind, driving me to my knees. The taste of dirt and blood fills my mouth.

"I warned you," Cash says, looming over me. "I fucking warned you to stay away."

A boot connects with my stomach, driving the air from my lungs. I double over, gasping. Through the ringing in my ears, I hear Savannah screaming, begging them to stop.

"Get her out of here," Cash orders.

"No! *Legion*!" Her voice is raw with panic. "Let me go! Let me GO!"

I try to stand, to reach her, but another blow lands on my back, sending me sprawling. The world tilts, goes fuzzy at the edges.

"You think you can just take what's ours?" Someone —Wyatt, I think—growls above me. "You think you're worthy of an Ashby?"

I spit blood onto the dirt. "She's not... property."

Wrong answer. A boot connects with my ribs, and I hear something crack. Pain explodes through my chest.

Through swollen eyes, I see Savannah fighting against Marcus and another man, kicking and clawing as they drag her toward a truck I hadn't even noticed, I was so focused on this woman.

"Legion!" She's sobbing now. "Don't hurt him! Please don't hurt him!"

I try to call her name, but all that comes out is a wet cough. More hands on me now, pinning me down. I buck against them, finding strength in desperation, but there are too many.

Something hard and heavy connects with the back of my head—a rock, maybe, or a pistol butt. Stars explode behind my eyes.

The last thing I hear is Savannah screaming my name as darkness swallows me whole.

END OF BOOK SHIT

Welcome to the End of Book shit. This is the part of the book where I get to say anything I want about the book you just read. Thoughts about what was on my mind, my plans, how it turned out, why I wrote it—stuff like that.

I started writing this novella serial series in April of 2025. The first pass went pretty quick and I had planned on writing six serial novellas and releasing during the summer. Maybe August. But then I sold my ranch in July, bought an RV, and traveled the country so… yeah. lol The best laid plans.

But I was smart enough to book narrators early – I think it was June—and it was Teddy Hamilton, so it was literally a 12-month wait.

12 months.

This was the second time in two months that I was told the wait was impossibly long. I had booked Jason Clarke just a couple weeks earlier for my dark mafia romance trilogy and that was a 9 month wait.

So all the work I did in early 2025 was pushed back for a 2026 release.

Knowing this was the case, I just… put Legion on the back burner. They weren't even going to record until early 2026, so I did other things. Wrote other books which will not have audiobooks releasing with them because again, waiting 12 months for a simultaneous ebook-paperback-audiobook release is fine for big projects—but it's really hard to pay the bills with traditional-publisher timelines on an indie-romance-author budget.

The bottleneck in audiobook production is real.

But then, after I parked my Winnebago, bought a new house, settled in… I started thinking that I wasn't going to wait to release Legion. I'm going to release in January 2026 as weekly serials, just as I planned.

Just to be clear, and to make sure everyone understands what I just said—these are SERIALS. If you're not sure what a serial is, allow me to explain. Every novella ends on a cliffhanger. It's like TV series. It has 'seasons' and it keeps going until it's cancelled.

This is how all my long series are structured with one exception - I tie each book up with a bow, end the 'romance' arc for the main couple of that book, then pick up the series with a new couple in the next book.

That's NOT what this series is. This is all about Legion and Savannah. Ups and down, ins and outs, and I'm not going to apologize for not tying it up in a bow.

Every novella in this series will have a cliffhanger.

Now, I'm releasing them weekly. This is no way implies that I'm WRITING them weekly. I've been working on this series - five novellas, 30-35K each, approx 164K words - for 8 months. Not full time. But I started writing these books 8 months ago.

Writing novellas is neither quick, nor easy. Please keep that in mind when you want to throw your Kindle against the wall because the next novella or omnibus isn't out yet.

Now… I do not mind people complaining about cliffhangers. It means they want more story. So, in my view, that's a good thing.

So… I hope we're all clear on what this is and what this isn't.

Anyway…

When I went back to editing it, I felt like it was only 5 novellas, so that's what it is. Five. It's 163,916 words so it's not short, that's for sure. When I first started thinking about Legion and Savannah—which was a couple of years ago now—it was going to be a massive dark family drama with bikers and ranchers.

Sons of Anarchy meets Yellowstone. If they had a baby raised by the devil himself.

And it's still very much that.

The original title of the book was Dust and Flowers, and that's still the title of the first novella.

So the first 'book' was always meant to be this long —163-ish,000 words.

All that came out just as I had imagined it would.

What changed was the release strategy. And by changed, I mean it was in place when I started writing, but it wasn't what I had imagined a couple years ago when I first came up with the plot.

The Serial Structure came later.

I've only seriously written one other serial, it was

the Social Media series in 2014. It was a massive success. I think, at one point, all six novellas were in the Top 100 at the same time. Massive, massive success.

But it was a lot of work, and I was releasing every two weeks back then. I did not write them ahead of time, it was all very rush, rush, rush. Too stressful.

I highly doubt readers have any idea how much the business of authoring has changed in the past few years. To be fair, I've been doing this almost 14 years now, and it's always changing, but the changes in the last two years are giving us whiplash.

Most of this is Amazon.

It's really hard to get their attention. Who knows what they like.

So we guess.

That's what my novella release is. A guess. I would not call it a gamble, it's going to pay out no matter what I do with it. I'm just trying to find my place in the new reality of AI we're all living in. So five weeks in a row, five new releases. I'm hoping for the Amazon algorithm love. At least a tiny bit of it.

So, I'm going to be very blunt and up front right now—I do not care if readers scream about cliffhangers. I do not care if they post comments that they're not gonna read it until "it's done"—I don't have the luxury of giving out fucks about shit I don't control.

This is my strategy for Legion.

5 novellas, one week apart.

In the summer, after waiting one year for the audiobook, I will release a 'season one' omnibus with the audio.

And then I'll release 'season two' the same way.

And season three. And four—if we get that far.

But it is what it is.

That's what I'm saying here.

I don't go on socials much anymore because all I see (especially in the book world) are people bitching and moaning about anything and everything. The reader complaints are spectacularly out of hand, the entitlement these same readers feel to the author's time is beyond the pale, and the return on investment that we authors get for trying to please people is never worth the abuse.

That's kind of what I think about the most vocal portion of the indie romance reader community these days. They are hungry for drama. They are drooling for controversy. They are just pulling on the leash, trying to find the next victim they can publicly shame, or tear apart, or ruin.

And I'm not here for it.

Read it.

Like it.

Hate it.

Whatever.

This is my art.

It feeds my soul, but it also pays my bills.

And I'm going to pay my bills no matter what anyone says about this book, these characters, or the release schedule.

I just cannot, and will not, factor in the dramatic opinions of entitled people when it comes to my soul. The world is crazy, times are changing, everything is in flux and I just don't have the time, the desire, or the stamina to conform to whatever 'reader expectations' are popular today.

This paperback was made for my annual 12 Days of Giveaways so I could give it out as one of the prizes.

It's also for my Patreon. They get all five novellas released at once in this omnibus format about 2 months early.

I'm sad that the audiobooks take so long these days. I've always had to wait for amazing narrators, but this is the longest wait ever and I've got over 100 audiobooks on audible.

So things have to change.

These stories were written six months ago now. Six months I've been sitting on a product because of the audiobook production bottleneck.

We're all just trying to survive.

And while I 100% do prefer releasing the ebook, audiobook, paperback at the same time, this audiobook bottleneck is making that strategy almost impossible unless you work for a year without pay.

As it is, indie authors, well, all authors, actually, get paid after the work is done. If you spend 6 months writing a book, you don't get paid for it until you spend all that time, plus money on an editor, cover designer, promotion etc – until TWO MONTHS AFTER THE BOOK RELEASES. Amazon pays out two months after you publish. You're always getting paid two months behind.

That's what—if it takes an author 6 months to write a book—that's about 10 months these authors work for free.

I don't take six months to write a book, but it's

always going to be four months of work, AT LEAST, for no pay.

You get NOTHING.

ZERO $$$.

Empty pockets.

This is how it is.

And then, once you get that book out, you've got the complainers demanding where book 2 is. Do these people even hear themselves?

I just saw a post a couple of days ago (it was in a LitRPG group, not romance, but the readers in that genre have the same tone-deaf small minority as the indie romance) and this guy wanted to know what all the writers are doing with their time, because they take so long between books. How dare these authors take a break.

I'll just say this right now, those people are not fans, they are trolls. And if I ever see a comment about me like that (which I probably never will, because I don't look at socials) but it would be an immediate block. That reader's contribution to my success isn't worth that kind of abuse.

It's just crazy that authors are working so hard, so many hours without pay, and readers just abuse them. Not only that, they feel it's RIGHT to abuse them.

And this abuse isn't framed as HATE. It's framed as LOVE. We love your book so much, write us more, more, more.

Let me just be clear here - I don't think my readers do that. If they do, it's not anywhere I can see it. My reader group on Facebook is perfect community of book lovers, if you ask me. But I've seen what the readers say to other writers. Like, in their groups. It's crazy.

Anyway, I'm sorry this EOBS is about the business of writing, but it needs to be said.

Misery loves company.

That's why these nasty readers stay nasty.

They are miserable people and want to make everyone around them miserable too.

And now we've got people faking drama to get sympathy sales.

I mean, what the fuck guys.

Why is the world so nuts?

Thankfully, I have cultivated a core group of fabulous readers around me and my stories. I see you, I love you, and I appreciate you!

Many, many fun things coming to Patreon this year!

And I will be releasing a lot of novellas.

Audiobooks, and omnibuses, and regular full-length trilogies too, don't worry. I'm not a 'serial author' now. I just need to find my new place in this new world emerging all around us and I'm going to be experimenting with shorter works and more consistent weekly, bi-weekly, and/or monthly releases to see what works best.

But my major new series for 2026 - DARK MAFIA ROMANCE - is on track, trilogy is written, going into audiobook production, or in production, and there will be a simultaneous release with ebook, audiobook, paperback in the spring of 2026.

So…

Thank you for reading, thank you for reviewing, and I'll see you in the next book.

Julie
JA Huss
November 11, 2025

P.S. (written February 10, 2026)

I've included a little bonus FBI Book Club. This is a joke I started putting in my newsletters about having my own FBI agent assigned to me due to my 'professional research'.

I won't have this in all the novellas (you'll see why) but there will be one in the last novella, Skulls and Lace, too. :)

AGENT MARSH
AGENT CASTILLO
AGENT DAVID
AGENT KAI
AGENT KOWALSKI
FBI

FBI BOOK CLUB — SUNDAY SCIF-CHAT
Assignment: *Dust and Flowers* (Book of Legion #1) by
JA Huss Transcript — CLASSIFIED
(it's not but Castillo insists)

[10:01 PM — AGENT: DAVID has started the meeting]
[10:01 PM — AGENT: KOWALSKI has entered the meeting]
[10:01 PM — AGENT: CASTILLO has entered the meeting]
[10:01 PM — AGENT: MARSH has entered the meeting]
[10:02 PM — AGENT: KAI has entered the meeting]

[10:02 PM — AGENT: KAI has enabled Profanity Filter: Auto-Emoji Mode]

David: Welcome back, everyone. Before we begin, I've appointed Kai as moderator and the new language filter has been enabled because last month's transcript was forwarded to the Deputy Director's office and I had to explain what "rearrange my guts" meant in a literary context. Also, just so everyone's aware, this call is [audio drops] ...internal affairs... [static] ...flagged for...

Castillo: Wait. Did he just say internal—

Kowalski: That is CENSORSHIP, David.

Castillo: —Kowalski, hold on, I think he said internal aff—

Kowalski: I will NOT survive this filter. I have not slept since I finished this book. I am unhinged. I am FERAL. I am in my villain era except the villain is a woman lying facedown on her bedroom floor thinking about a man whose mother named him after a BIBLICAL DEMON POSSESSION VERSE and I need everyone on this call to understand I am NOT ✺✺✺ing OKAY—

David: See? The filter works fine.

Kai: It works great. Hey, Kowalski — you know what else is fine? The way you get when you're all worked up about a book. I want to stick my fingers in your pussy, pin you against a wall with my dick, and hear you moan my name the way Savannah says Leg—

Kowalski: ...👀
David: ...👀
Marsh: ...👀

Castillo: …The filter doesn't catch that?

Kai: It was supposed to catch that.

David: It catches PROFANITY, Kai. Not— whatever THAT was.

Kai: I need a different filter.

[10:08 PM — AGENT: KAI has enabled REDACTION FILTER: BookTok Mode]

Kai: Testing. Kowalski, I want to 🤏🍆💦 you until you 😰😩 and then 🔥👅 —

David: KAI.

Kai: What? It's all emojis now. Nobody knows what that means.

Kowalski: EVERYBODY knows what that means.

Kai: Then everybody has great taste. Can we talk about the book?

David: We are NEVER discussing this again. Let's talk about the book. I thought Dust and Flowers was a grounded, mature exploration of class dynamics in rural Montana—

Kowalski: CLASS DYNAMICS? He strung fairy lights in an abandoned grain silo and waited at midnight for her to gallop bareback through a creek bed on a half-million-dollar horse. He made DIRT sacred, David. I want to bite that man on his freshly branded chest and I am not being metaphorical.

David: …Let's start with the opening. Cash picks Legion up from Whitefall, delivers a warning, and leaves him stranded on the highway. I thought Cash raised some valid—

Marsh: Don't say valid.

David: He's protecting his sister from a convicted criminal.

Castillo: He transported Legion under false pretenses and abandoned him forty miles from the nearest settlement in extreme heat without means of communication. Montana Code 45-5-302. Reckless endangerment at minimum.

David: He gave him a ride.

Castillo: He gave him a psychological operation with leather seats. I've also been mapping the route. Based on described landmarks and driving time from Whitefall to Drybone—

Kowalski: Castillo, are you on Google Earth right now? Castillo: I am conducting geographic verification relevant to the incident file.

Kowalski: We don't HAVE an incident file.

Castillo: The Badlands MC compound sits approximately six miles southeast of Terry, Montana. Property off Highway 253. Correct acreage, sight lines to the Yellowstone River valley, access to the Terry Badlands formation. I have coordinates. 46.7918° N, 105.2847° W.

Kowalski: You GPS'd the fictional clubhouse.

Castillo: The author provides extremely detailed geographic data. I would be negligent not to cross-reference.

Kowalski: Negligent to WHOM?

Castillo: To the process, Kowalski.

David: MOVING ON. Cash shows Legion a staged engagement photo and tells him Savannah called their relationship "a phase." I think that's a fair characterization—

Kowalski: A PHASE? They've been meeting at that silo for SIX YEARS. Childhood sweethearts. Secret relationship. Forbidden love across a class divide that makes the Montagues and Capulets look like a HOA dispute. That is not a phase. That is an ✿✿✿ing INEVITABILITY and I want to climb Legion Kane like the grain silo he decorated for her.

Marsh: Kowalski, from a clinical perspective, you are describing a trauma bond with a fictional character.

Kowalski: I am describing LOVE, Marsh. Raw. Feral. Down-bad-since-fourteen love. He carved their initials in a tree at fifteen and she VIOLENTLY crossed them out while he was in prison because "he makes her sad" and STILL brought groceries to his nine-year-old sister twice a month. That's not a trauma bond. That's a 🌸🌸 🌸ing VOCATION.

David: Can we talk about Marcus?

Castillo: Can we not.

David: Georgetown-educated. Politically connected. Offering Savannah stability and—

Kowalski: He calls her follower count "rural demographic reach." That's not a fiancé. That's a campaign manager with a ring budget.

David: He's under stress. The bikers crashed his—

Castillo: An entire MC executed a coordinated tactical formation up a private driveway during a political event with a sitting senator present. Zero weapons discharged. Textbook disruption op.

Kowalski: Most romantic thing I've ever read.

Castillo: Those aren't mutually exclusive and that concerns me.

David: Then Marcus pushes Savannah and she falls, and honestly that's nothing compared to what he does in Book—

[CONTENT REDACTED BY MODERATOR: KAI]

David: —if you think the push is bad—

[CONTENT REDACTED BY MODERATOR: KAI]

Kowalski: David. Did you read ahead?

Kai: He read ahead.

David: Anyway. CHAPTER 6. The silo reunion.

Kowalski: She strips. Removes the ring. Blue cotton dress. Cassia bareback through the creek at midnight. JUMPS A FIVE-RAIL FENCE. Sheds every fake layer on the ride there. He's in the doorway bathed in golden light like a fallen angel who knows how to hang fairy lights and I want him to 🌶️🤚🍑 me against that wall and 🍑👅 until I 😰😩 and then 🍆💦😵 me—

[10:25 PM — AGENT: KAI has disabled REDACTION FILTER: BookTok Mode]

Kowalski: —pinning me against that silo wall with those dirty fucking hands, Legion, pull my hair and tell me I'm yours, make me feel it for DAYS, I don't care about the ring or the ranch or the shotguns, I want your mouth on my pussy, making it all wet and squishy—

David: … 👀
Marsh: … 👀
Castillo: … 👀
Kai: … 👀

Kowalski: Why is everyone quiet?

Marsh: Filter's off.

Kowalski: SINCE WHEN?

Kai: "and then 🍆🔥😵 me—"

Kowalski: KAI.

Kai: What? I wanted to hear it.

[10:28 PM — AGENT: KAI has re-enabled REDACTION FILTER: BookTok Mode]

Castillo: I've mapped the bareback route. Three point seven miles, eastern pasture, creek bed crossing. The silo matches a decommissioned grain elevator visible on satellite since 2011. I have coordinates.

Kowalski: We are discussing the most emotionally devastating reunion 🌶 scene in dark romance history and you are on GOOGLE EARTH?

Castillo: The forty-seven thousand acres with artesian wells and Yellowstone River valley views corresponds to a specific corridor in Prairie County. The dry riverbed separating Kane and Ashby land places the silo at approximately—

Kowalski: You are GPS'ing the 🌱 silo.

Castillo: It's a GRAIN silo with forensic significance. The Badlands compound sits six miles southeast of Terry off Highway 253. 46.7918° N, 105.2847° W. Give or take.

David: Castillo, we've talked about this. You cannot investigate fiction.

Castillo: The author provides extremely detailed geographic data. I would be negligent not to cross-reference.

David: Chapter 7. Legion tells Savannah she's "allowed" to marry Marcus and sends her back. I think that shows real matur—

Kowalski: MATURITY? He told the love of his life to marry someone else because he thinks he's too broken to deserve her. He watched her ride away on her expensive horse back to her mansion and convinced himself it was over. That's not maturity. That's a martyr complex wearing a leather cut and I am 💀😩🖤 GUTTED. He doesn't think he's worthy. He is WRONG and I want to 💋🥩🍖 him and then 🍆🥒😵 him until he UNDERSTANDS.

Marsh: From a psychological standpoint, Legion exhibits classic patterns of internalized unworthiness stemming from—

Kowalski: He's a cinnamon roll who thinks he's a villain.

Marsh: …Reductive but not inaccurate.

David: The branding ceremony. Chapter 8. Can we discuss it professionally?

Kowalski: No.

David: Capital B. Hot iron. Full membership witnessing. He earns his cut after three years of silent prison time.

Castillo: Aggravated assault with a deadly weapon, even with consent. Every brother present is an accessory.

Kowalski: He didn't make a sound.

Castillo: That's not legally relevant.

Kowalski: It's 🖤🔥💀 relevant. He let them burn belonging into his chest without flinching because that's what family costs in his world. Legion Kane has never had anything that was truly his except pain and Savannah and now this brand and I am 😖😰😵 — I need to lie down. I need to lie down on the FLOOR. He is touch her and die, property of, morally gray, obsessed MMC, only-her-for-twelve-years PERFECTION and I am not surviving this series. I am 💀. I am DECEASED. Bury me in the silo.

Kai: Kowalski.

Kowalski: WHAT.

Kai: …Breathe.

Kowalski: …

Kowalski: Thank you.

David: Then Mercy. He finds his nine-year-old sister asleep in his bed clutching a BB gun. She asks if the club will help find Destiny. He promises. Kids at school call him "Demon Kane" and cite Mark 5:9 as proof. And he tells Mercy his demons will protect her.

Kowalski: Which is the single most devastating found family moment I have ever read. He is in physical AGONY from the brand and his baby sister asks him for a promise and he makes it without hesitating. I am not okay. I will never be okay again. DNR. Do not resuscitate. Let me 💀.

David: I was going to say it was well-written.

Kowalski: It's not "well-written," David. It's a WAR CRIME against my emotions.

Castillo: Speaking of the child. Nine years old. Alone in a condemned trailer for two months. Malnourished. Nonverbal. Armed with a Red Ryder. Emerges from a juniper bush like—and I'm quoting—"a wild thing." This is a CPS emergency.

Marsh: And yet the only person consistently providing her with food and clean clothes is Savannah Ashby. Twice a month, the actual ranch heiress drives to Kane scrubland to feed this child. No one asked her to. No one knows. She just does it. That's who Savannah is underneath seventy thousand photographs.

David: Savannah is engaged to Marcus.

Kowalski: Savannah is engaged to a PRESS RELEASE, David. She removes that ring like it's burning her before she even gets on the horse. Wrong ring on her finger is the trope and she KNOWS it.

David: I just think we should respect the engagement as a legitimate—

Kai: David, she told him to claim her and make her remember she's his. That's not a woman who respects her engagement. That's a thesis statement.

David: Chapter 9. The club bought Legion a new double-wide trailer with three years of pooled contributions while he was in prison. And Mercy's reaction—

Kowalski: Don't.

David: She cries and says "good things don't happen to me."

Kowalski: I SAID DON'T. 🫣 💀

Castillo: The financial logistics interest me. Forty-seven patched members contributing over thirty-six months. That's approximately fourteen dollars per member per month for a manufactured home in that price range. Surprisingly reasonable community investment. Possibly tax-deductible if they structured it as—

Marsh: Castillo.

Castillo: I'm just saying the brotherhood operates a more effective mutual aid network than most government programs.

David: Chapter 10. The underground vault. Hidden elevator in her closet. Forty feet down. Climate-controlled archive. A red leather album of photographs of Legion spanning his entire life — toddler to adulthood. Increasingly intimate. And the final photo — a selfie of Eleanor and twenty-four-year-old Legion in a truck, both smiling, six months before she died.

Castillo: Twenty-plus years of documentation of a

minor by a woman in a position of social power. Portraits described as "increasingly naked." A vault designed to conceal the collection. This is not a portfolio. This is evidence.

David: Eleanor was a respected—

Kai: Eleanor was a predator with a Leica and a trust fund, David.

Castillo: And her will explicitly excludes Legion from the family she spent two decades photographing him into. That's not a will. That's a restraining order from the grave.

Kowalski: And Savannah finds this book and looks at every page and locks it away and never confronts him. She carries it ALONE. Because she loves him more than she needs answers. 🖤

Marsh: That's avoidant attachment manifesting as—

Kowalski: That is DEVOTION, Marsh.

David: Chapter 11. Mercy shows Savannah the new trailer. And this is where we see the MC teaching Mercy. Brick brings candy. Roach teaches chess and how to check for break-ins. Ledger brings math workbooks. Diesel teaches shooting. Chains draws her pictures. Butch teaches her to punch. Ratchet shows her vehicle maintenance.

Kowalski: Dangerous men with felony records teaching a nine-year-old tactical skills alongside genuine kindness. Mercy got SUSPENDED for punching a boy who called Legion "Demon Kane" and BRICK APPROVED. I would 💀 for every single one of these men and I need each of them to get a book.

David: Well, actually—

[CONTENT REDACTED BY MODERATOR: KAI]

David: I was just—

[CONTENT REDACTED BY MODERATOR: KAI]

Kowalski: WHY does Kai keep censoring you?

David: No reason. Chapter 12.

Kai: He knows something.

David: I know NOTHING. Chapter 12. The confrontation. The ultimatum.

Kowalski: 💀🖤🔥😭 I cannot. I CANNOT. She shows up wearing Marcus's ring and Legion tells her she lost the right to ask about his family when she put on another man's diamond. And she says she's loved him since she was TWELVE. And she offers to walk away from EVERYTHING. Forty-seven thousand acres. The horses. The inheritance. ALL OF IT. And he says NO. Because he can't support them with a prison record and he won't abandon Mercy and he won't leave his twenty acres of scrubland. He would rather she be SAFE AND MISERABLE than free and his. I have seen God and God is a tattooed ex-con choosing a woman's suffering over his own happiness because he thinks he's not enough and I need MEDICAL ATTENTION—

David: It's a reasonable economic—

Kowalski: "Your cage is better than my freedom." That's what he's saying. And she's saying "I'd rather have your dust than their diamonds" and NEITHER WILL BUDGE and this is the most 🖤😣💀😨 thing ever committed to a page. Second chance. Forbidden love. Rich girl poor boy. Impossible choice. Only her for TWELVE YEARS. I am having a RELIGIOUS EXPERIENCE. I am SPEAKING IN TROPES. I will never read another book. Every book after this is just paper. I am RUINED. Legion Kane has ruined me for all fictional men and most real ones and I am 💀 💀 💀 DECEASED. Legion Kane has ruined me for all fictional men and most real ones and I am UNWELL and UNMEDICATED and I do NOT want the cure. 3-5 business days before I can function—

David: And then she tells him midnight.

Kowalski: And he goes. Because he has never. Been able. To refuse her. And they're against the silo wall and it's desperate and claiming and 👅💦😢 and then 🍆🔥 🫠 —

David: And then the flashlights.

Kowalski: …
Marsh: …

Castillo: I have notes on this.

David: Cash. Wyatt. Marcus. Ranch hands with guns.

Kowalski: They catch them. Mid— they catch them TOGETHER and rip him away from her and—

Castillo: Aggravated assault. Unlawful restraint. Conspiracy. Armed ranch hands constituting a paramilitary formation against a single unarmed individual during a consensual encounter. Minimum seven felonies. I haven't finished the scene breakdown.

Kowalski: They beat him UNCONSCIOUS. While she screams. While she fights and claws and BEGS. Someone hits him in the back of the head and the last thing he hears is her screaming his name and then DARKNESS. And it ENDS. It just ENDS. Dirt. Blood. Her voice breaking on his name. I want to every Ashby brother with their own shotguns—

David: It's a cliffhanger. Serials do that.

Kowalski: It's not a CLIFFHANGER, David. It's a CRIME against my . I am a before and an after and the dividing line is Legion Kane unconscious in Montana dirt. I NEED BOOK TWO IMMEDIATELY.

David: Well—

Kowalski: Do NOT tell me to wait for next week's assignment.

David: I was going to say the serial structure is effective—

Kowalski: You're being weirdly calm about this ending.

Kai: Suspiciously calm.

David: I'm a measured reader.

Kowalski: You CRIED during Colleen Hoover.

David: That was allergies.

Castillo: You defended Marcus for forty-five minutes without raising your voice. Your baseline agitation on book club calls is significantly higher. You're either medicated or you know something.

Marsh: … 👀
Castillo: … 👀
Kai: … 👀
Kowalski: … 👀

David: …Fine. I read all five.

Kowalski: YOU—

David: One sitting. Eleven PM to six AM last Tuesday. I have been PRETENDING to be objective this entire call and I can't do it anymore because Marcus is not— he's so much WORSE and what he does to Savannah—

[CONTENT REDACTED BY MODERATOR: KAI]

David: —and BRICK, Brick is NOT who you think—

[CONTENT REDACTED BY MODERATOR: KAI]

David: —and the VOTE, oh God, when Legion has to—

[CONTENT REDACTED BY MODERATOR: KAI]

David: KAI STOP CENSORING ME—

Kai: NO SPOILERS. YOUR OWN RULE.

David: MY RULE IS STUPID. THESE PEOPLE NEED TO KNOW.

Kowalski: ⚔️🔪🖤💀😩😨 WHAT HAPPENS TO LEGION? DAVID. IS HE OKAY? DOES HE—

[CONTENT REDACTED BY MODERATOR: KAI]

David: KAI.

Kai: You'll thank me later.

David: Let me say ONE thing. Not a spoiler. An opinion.

Kai: …One thing.

David: I was wrong about Marcus.

Marsh: … 👀
Castillo: … 👀
Kai: … 👀
Kowalski: … 👀

David: I was wrong about Marcus and I was wrong about Legion. There is a moment — I won't say when — where Legion does something so quietly selfless it broke every framework I had for who he is. I've been defending the wrong man this entire call.

Marsh: David?

David: I'm embarrassed. I sat here championing financial stability while this man — this man with twenty-seven dollars and a demon's name—

Kowalski: David. Are you crying?

David: I have ALLERGIES.

Castillo: It is February in an indoor facility.

David: I have INDOOR allergies.

Kowalski: The book broke David. 💀 💀 💀 💀 💀 THE BOOK BROKE DAVID. This is the greatest day of my LIFE.

Kai: For the record, I also read ahead. Finished all five Thursday night.

Kowalski: WHAT 🔪 ⚔️ 💀

Castillo: …I may have acquired the remaining installments. For geographic verification.

Kowalski: EVERYONE READ AHEAD EXCEPT ME??? 😩 ⚔️ 🖤 🔪 💀 😰 🥴 I am being VICTIMIZED by this book club. I am the ONLY person suffering in real time. This is a HATE CRIME against my 🖤—

Marsh: I DNF'd after Book 3 because the psychological implications of—

[CONTENT REDACTED BY MODERATOR: KAI]

Marsh: Oh, come ON.

David: Official position. Book 2 next week. Nobody spoils. Nobody Google Earths.

Castillo: The Google Earth window stays open. The cottonwood tree line is visible in satellite imagery. I've matched the grain elevator. Decommissioned since 2011.

David: We don't need incident mapping. OK, that's it people! Same time next week.

Kowalski: I'm reading it TONIGHT. I am going to 📖🔪 🌶🖤💀😩😰 my way through all four remaining books and come back WEAPONIZED.

Castillo: Filing a geographic addendum.

Kai: Blood in.

[10:54 PM — AGENT: DAVID has ended the meeting]

[10:55 PM — AGENT: KOWALSKI has restarted the meeting without David]

Kowalski: He's gone. Who's telling me what happens to Legion? 🔪🔪🔪🔪

Castillo: 46.7918° N, 105.2847° W. Start there.

Kai: Nobody tell her. She needs to read it.

Kowalski: Kai I SWEAR 🗡🔪🔪👊🎤—

Kai: Read it. Trust me.

Kowalski: …Fine. But if he 💀 I'm transferring field offices. And burning this one down. 🔥🔥🔥🔥🔥

Kai: He doesn't—

[CONTENT REDACTED BY MODERATOR: KAI]

Kai: I just censored myself. I need to go to bed.

[11:01 PM — AGENT: KOWALSKI has ended the meeting]

[11:01 PM — SCIF-CHAT AUTO-SUMMARY: MEETING TRANSCRIPT COMPILED]

Book of Legion - Badlands MC #2
BLOOD
& grace
New York Times Bestselling Author
JA HUSS

They were caught at the silo at midnight.
Same place they've been hookin' up for years.
Her family thought violence would be enough to end it.
They were wrong.
It only made the bond stronger.
Outlaw clubhouse.
Public claiming.
Loyalty test.
Church At Dawn.

BLOOD AND GRACE

Down on your knees—it's time to choose sides.

ABOUT THE AUTHOR

JA Huss writes exclusively in coffee shops, where she orders oat milk lattes and journals about gratitude. She has a degree in something fun and breezy, lives in a charming walkable city with her hypoallergenic dog, and describes herself as "such a people person." She only reads rom-coms, has never once googled anything disturbing for research, and her browser history is immaculate. She does not own weapons, has never been to a gun range "just for fun," and has absolutely no opinions about federal agencies. She trusts all official narratives, has never tracked a flight, and thinks people who buy silver are "a little much." She does not run her own servers. She doesn't even know what a server is. She stores all her passwords in a Google doc labeled "passwords" like a normal person. She has never written a book about AI becoming sentient, has no theories about ancient civilizations, and did not homeschool her children out of distrust for institutions —she just thought it would be "a fun bonding experience." She has never referred to the FDA as "those people", does not pay for everything in cash and thinks that's a weird thing to do.

. . .

She writes light, wholesome fiction your mother would enjoy.